A WOMAN of SINGULAR OCCUPATION

ALSO BY PENELOPE GILLIATT

Novels

One By One
A State of Change
The Cutting Edge
Mortal Matters

Short Stories

Come Back If It Doesn't Get Better
Nobody's Business
Splendid Lives
Quotations From Other Lives
They Sleep Without Dreaming

Screenplay

Sunday Bloody Sunday

Stage Play

Property

Profiles and Criticism

Three-Quarter Face
Unholy Fools
Renoir: Essays, Conversations, Reviews
Jacques Tati

Penelope Gilliatt

A WOMAN of SINGULAR OCCUPATION

CHARLES SCRIBNER'S SONS   NEW YORK

Gilliatt
Pen

This is a work of fiction. Names, characters, places, and incidents are
either the product of the author's imagination or are used fictitiously.
Any resemblance to actual events or persons, living or dead, is entirely
coincidental.

Copyright © 1988 by Penelope Gilliatt

Charles Scribner's Sons
Macmillan Publishing Company
866 Third Avenue, New York, N.Y. 10022

Library of Congress Cataloging-in-Publication Data
Gilliatt, Penelope.
    A woman of singular occupation / by Penelope Gilliatt.
        p.   cm.
    ISBN 0-684-19072-9
    I. Title.
    PR6057.I58W6 1989
    823'.914–dc19   88-13928
                                                                    CIP

10 9 8 7 6 5 4 3 2 1

Printed in the United States of America

for Nolan
and
for Sophie

I thank for their professional help many people of knowledge and wisdom, including Baron Frederick de Testa; Jason Bacon; Numan Hazar; Professor Robert Caxton; Professor George Ivan Smith; Ben Sonnenberg; Alexandre de Gramont; Michael J. Arlen; Costa and Lydia Carras; Moshe Mizrahi; the late Janet Flanner; archivists of Free French, Vichy, and Turkish documents; and the librarians of the London Library, the Waldheim Research Studies of New York Central Library, and the Paris Bibliothèque Nationale.

P. G.

A WOMAN of SINGULAR OCCUPATION

1

♦

CATHERINE de Rochefauld climbed aboard the Simplon–Orient Express in Paris at the Gare de l'Est. Half-French, half-English, bound for Istanbul on July 15, 1939. Her husband's driver, a Turk, found her the reserved seat, saw to the tapestry-covered bags.

"An alarming Bastille Day," Mehmed said with distaste in Turkish. "May I have a word, madame? And the mood of yesterday: madame agrees?"

Catherine had her usual recoil from his unctuousness. She looked round for space for them to talk alone, saw a table in the empty *wagon-restaurant* ahead and sat down with him there, ordering them both a Perrier and writing him some reminder notes on a pad.

"I was wondering, madame, if I could shortly come home with you," he said.

"You should stay with monsieur in Paris. It's a disturbing time for diplomats. He'll be leaving soon," she said, keeping to Turkish for him.

He avoided her eye, as ever, and said, "The atmosphere, madame. Bastille Day is a French occasion. The English flag was everywhere yesterday."

"Have you been convinced by the fascist columnists?"

"This is a French occasion, madame. Not English."

"Don't tell me you're anti-English as well. You don't really like the French either, do you? Except"—she looked for a way to put it—"as part of the discipline of your work for monsieur."

"It is not for France to invite her dangerous beleaguered enemy since time immemorial. England's entente is not so long. I have in mind the Normans." He cracked his fingers. "And the Führer will be furious."

There is no language, she thought, speaking many herself, no language at all, in which that last sentence can be said. She ordered more Perrier. "Hitler," she said, "has been saying that his patience is exhausted ever since he decided to own Europe. He has a very low patience threshold. Bastille Day yesterday was serious simply because he has been furious, as you say, for ages. So far as ceremonial days can ever be serious. They're generally the days when students put colored inks into fountains."

"I beg your pardon," he said, with his way of making one feel that he should always be the one to grant the pardon.

"One of the points of the Bastille Day review was to show the Führer that two great European countries are ready to defend liberty. The French hope that the Germans can understand plain English."

"For myself, madame, I feel that Mr. Churchill's vigor, shall we say, may be a dangerous avoirdupois."

She saw the key at last: that he was very frightened. She laughed, to give him the ease of feeling that his joke had gone down well. "You'll be home, believe me, in two weeks at the most. Hold on. Monsieur needs you. He leans on you a great deal. Stand by him, Mehmed. Remember that Turkey is safe. Remember that she has a Declaration of Security with the English now."

He bowed his head. She smiled at him again, handing

him a note for her husband. "You should be off. The train's about to go. He'll see that you get home. He understands."

Mehmed bowed from the hips. Many a time she had longed to ask Jean-Pierre to find someone else. But the immaculate Jean-Pierre always said that Mehmed "understands my clothes too well for me to lose him."

"Well, madame, we are in the safe hands of Mr. Daladier, yes?" said Mehmed, standing.

She smiled again. "Except that he hasn't governed properly for donkeys' years."

With Mehmed gone, she went back to her seat. A hand waved to her from the platform. Ann Wisner's. An American friend married to a Turkish merchant. All the way to Istanbul with Ann: she braced herself, and waved back. Ann climbed aboard packed like a mule. "My dear, how wonderful," she shouted as she scrambled along the corridor. She sat down. Even in the vastness of the plumply upholstered berth that she was obviously meaning to share with Catherine, her mule panniers made indents in any neighbor. Her Worth pockets were bulging with what turned out to be cans of beef, candles, jars of cling peaches, cakes of soap.

"It seemed wise. I talked to my dear Kemal in Istanbul last night. In code, of course," she said at the top of her husky voice. "And he indicated preparedness."

"In the shape of cling peaches, though?"

"I caught the tone of a merchant's wisdom."

Catherine deflected any need for an answer with a smile and took out a book from her traveling bag. Ann Wisner poked her head into the bag. "Nothing forgotten. Laissez-passer; and I see the intriguing Paisley notebook. Ecstasy! You've brought your dumb keyboard. So if I shut my eyes I can imagine your music all the way through the waits at the frontiers. Why *do* we take this train." She looked at the brass fittings, the polished mahogany, the ease of the wondrous express.

"You must play your poor gagged marvels and I shall imagine Mozart," she said.

"Not now. The keyboard's with us only in case I can't get back to Paris."

"I'll hold it, you practice."

"It would get in everyone's way. The train's going to be packed. People are leaving Paris in hordes."

"You wouldn't give us something to imagine even if I hold the weight safely while you play? My darling Catherine, what gifts. A composer on the quiet, a friend beyond compare, the perfect diplomat's wife. And such a dresser. How do you afford the time to shop?"

Catherine wondered where to begin answering, if at all, and simply said again, "I shan't be practicing. You won't have to imagine interminable scales." She climbed up on the seat to reach the luggage rack and lodged her dumb keyboard between suitcases. "And as to the candles, what was it your husband said?"

"He just told me to bring everything we might need in extremity. Those were his words. Spooky." Ann Wisner, for all her lithe American looks, had the beginning of jowls, and she shook them periodically in happy anticipation of the face-lift she so often spoke of having.

"Everything we might need," said Catherine. The impossibility of it.

"I kept the provisions to picnic style. Heaven knows, we are going to be in the Balkans. And when do you think war will be declared? Kemal put it at ten days' time." Ann produced a salami sausage in Worth couture wrapping paper, looked at it, and said, "May we put it beside your keyboard?"

Catherine stood on her toes on the train seat to make a distant place for the sausage. "Anything else?"

"Your wonderful ankles, Catherine! Yes, perhaps this goat's cheese, it's beginning to smell already. One does dislike the smell of dairy products on clothes. That is to say, if goats be dairy. If goats are dairy." Ann pummeled cushions as she rattled on. She was able to sleep at any time, and Catherine remembered this faculty thankfully. Her friend (yes, she was that: totally constant, and only garrulous because she was as frightened as most people on the train) would soon drift away into a doze. Even her slumbering small presence was comforting. She had a face like an Austin Seven. Her manner indicated nothing about her gentle attention. A useful mask in wartime, thought Catherine, who had learned over the years in Istanbul that her friend had a deal of wisdom below the girlish gush. Her chattiness might lead crowds of people to think they knew her, but only a few friends had any notion of her fine grain. Surprising lady. She went to sleep as the train jerked to a start. Catherine read for an hour and then went into the corridor with her fingers in her book to walk about, peering into the men's smoking lounge, her favorite of the train's odd pleasures. Its replicas of bygone comforts perhaps reflected no historical reality at all. The Orient Express nourished myths. She could see in the smoking room a man in a deer stalker, smoking a curl-handled pipe. Only the Orient Express could give birth to its own Sherlock Holmes.

She put her head in.

"This is reserved for men, madame," he said in bad French.

"Sorry," she said in English.

"Oh good, you're English. It's raining, isn't it. Daresay French gardens need it. Must remind you of home."

She smiled and closed the forbidden door. One day it

must be possible to say that rain also reminded her of Paris.

"It's raining," said a handsome young American in the corridor. "I could hear your British accent. It must remind you of home."

"No, of Paris." She grinned, and passed by him. A little further along she turned the beautiful engraved handle of what turned out to be a cloakroom. Before the door was quickly slammed, she had had a glimpse of a man doing something with bottles of liquid to a passport in the wash-basin. She had been seen, and her face had registered. On her way back she had to control herself from shivering. The young American, eager, polite, even tried to make peacetime conversation with her about having a game of tennis with him, waving his briefcase in a mime of an ace serve. He was in banking, he said. His name was Thomas Drake, he said.

"I'm going to a job in Istanbul." He produced a card with a telephone number.

"I've got a place there on the Bosphorus. Ramshackle."

"Could I call you up?"

"There aren't many private telephones in Istanbul. I'm in the Ankara directory under my husband's name. Jean-Pierre de Rochefauld." That brilliant smile.

*F*rontier inspections in Italy, in Belgrade, where sleepers from Berlin were unsettlingly allowed to join the sumptuous train, although the Orient Express's direct route through Germany was already being eliminated. The train had been crammed since the South of France with families carrying cardboard suitcases and hastily packed bundles of belongings wrapped in pillowcases fixed to the ends of poles. Ann Wisner asked Catherine to climb up to the rack. "A slice of the salami," she said happily, inspired by the sight of refugees with napkins spread over their chests, elaborately ceremonial over minor national snacks. In each case the oldest woman of the family was cutting up bread or a chicken with a penknife. Catherine watched. "Always toward the chest," she said out loud without thinking. To Ann: "We should keep the salami for later. We might as well have binges in the *wagon-restaurant* until it's uncoupled." They stood in the corridor and waited for a lunch table. The maître d'hôtel of the *wagon-restaurant* seated them with a bow. He was still in a tailcoat, the china still Dresden, the wine list still impeccable. Hitler might never have existed.

"All refugees, were they, back in the compartment?" said Ann in what she supposed to be a low voice. Refugees were trying to sleep in the corridor now.

"Anti-Fascists. Jews. Anyone against Pétain and Laval."

"Not loyal Frenchmen, you mean?"

Catherine crumbled some bread.

"That smile of yours, dear. It spreads such a hush." Pause. "Am I waking anyone? Oh, and did you mean *we're* not loyal? Not to be staying in Paris?"

"We're perfectly loyal. Your husband's Turkish, my husband's posted to Turkey in the French foreign service. None of us could be called flitters."

"Loyal diplomat, loyal trader, loyal wives," said Ann. "But we are flitting. We're leaving for somewhere safer. There's no getting round it. Dear Catherine, are you privately quitting Pétain? When you're as old as I am—no. I'll speak about that another time. Well, I can't resist a hint. My *cinq-à-sept* in Paris . . . And who knows what he will feel about me after my face-lift."

Dear Ann. She chattered on. "You *are* on the side of Pétain, aren't you? Like your husband?"

7

"But of *course,* as he would say."

"One can have separate love affairs without doing damage to the marriage, but political opinions are in the man's hands, my darling Kemal says."

"Yes, and women have babies in hedges."

Ann said, "As an American I know what you mean, but I can't let myself joke about women's place with Kemal. He gets troubled. How does Jean-Pierre react to jokes?" It was hospitably asked, as if she were wondering whether he were allergic to shellfish. "Does he joke? What language?"

"If he feels particularly distinct, which in Jean-Pierre's case comes out as wit, he uses French."

"Yes. French is such a distinct language," said Ann.

They went back to their compartment. Ann bent over Catherine's book. "What are you reading? Oh, it's French. How I envy you. I've got the most atrocious accent."

"But you speak beautiful Turkish."

"And what's the book? *'Le fil de'*—what's *'l'épée'*?"

" *'The Edge of the Sword.'* It's about kinds of militarism, or maybe ideals of national loyalty, written by de Gaulle with a salute to Pétain. It's apparently caused a lot of trouble between them. Salutes can. In the Great War Papa had a private who hated the sergeant major. He thumbed his nose at him when he was supposed to be saluting. He said, 'My hand slipped down my face on account of it got lost in admiration, sir.' "

Pause. Ann nearly understood, and fought gamely back to her point. "De Gaulle used to worship Pétain, and now he seems to detest him."

"He trained him. They were both prize products of the same military academy, yes? Saint-Cyr? They have everything in common," said Catherine.

"He calls him *mon vieux.*"

"Or *le vieux,* is it?" said Catherine. Hang on to vagueness. Play the Turkish wife of old. The fez and the veil might have gone but remember again that such things were still a man's business, according to the rules required of Ann.

"It is what we should do, isn't it? Hold out for Pétain? Better than Laval," said Ann.

Divert, said Catherine to herself. There were too many people ready to eavesdrop in this compartment. "I leave politics to Jean-Pierre."

"So why are you reading '*Le Fil de*' whatever?"

"I got misled by the title. I thought it was going to be a good thriller for a train journey." Catherine could play the flapper girl if she wanted.

"Is it true that de Gaulle is obsessed with the importance of tanks?"

"Maybe I skipped that. There's something here about using pigeons as code-message carriers in times of crisis."

"You like that, of course, your father always having been such a bird fancier." Ann looked down the corridor and said, "I'm surprised you skipped the tanks. Being half-English, and tanks being an English invention. Were you a Girl Guide?"

"Girl Guides don't do engineering. It's mostly knots."

"No, but these things lead to—well, they lead to other things, don't they," said Ann. After another endless frontier inspection had passed, Ann said, "I do want to pick your brains while we're alone together. In Istanbul I have to go straight in for the face-lift—if the surgeons are still attending properly in this crisis, which one can only hope—and you and I may not have a chance like this again. You're such a fount. To come straight to the point again, and I'm going to blow my nose because of your worry about being overheard, you *do* feel we should hold out for Pétain?"

Catherine said confidingly, seeing that talk was inevitable and had best be given the tone of women's gossip, "Someone who should know told me that he's a secret joker. He says he favors suspending the French parliament for the duration of the War, as and when it comes. He has explained himself to be humorous."

"The marshal said that?"

"He says that government is a frivolous parasite in war."

"Well, I don't understand, do you?"

"Not a word."

A couple who had been on the train since Paris had some bread.

"Ah, the last French bread," said Ann, as if that were the end of everything.

Catherine said, "But Turkish bread to come, and how I like trains."

"You're a loner, aren't you?"

Catherine smiled and shook her head. "No more than everyone else."

"Isn't that difficult for a diplomat husband? The entertaining?"

"I hope not."

"I couldn't help noticing from your labels that you're going to the house in Istanbul. You're not traveling on to the embassy in Ankara?"

"I rather badly want to be by the Bosphorus."

"With your beautiful instruments. Your harpsichord."

There was a respite of several hours while Ann slept. Then Catherine woke her and said, "Ann, we might as well try to get a dinner table. They unhitch the *wagon-restaurant* soon."

Darkness began to fall as they had dinner. When they walked back to the compartment it smelled of garlic, the

residue of many picnic meals. Dozing people held identifica-
tion papers and passports in their fists. Ann went to sleep
again, winding a bandage under her jaw and over the top of
her head as her nightly precaution against a double chin, and
waved good night. Catherine went out into the corridor after
a time and read by torchlight, this time a romance about
Anne Boleyn for the benefit of anyone watching. It sent her to
sleep almost immediately. After who knows how long,
Thomas's voice woke her. "Do you always sleep standing up?
Like a horse?"

She smiled and shook her hair to waken herself, looking
more beautiful than ever, and said, "Sorry I'm tired. The
journey's endless, isn't it?"

Thomas said, "A game of squash is what I need."

"There are good courts in Istanbul, as you probably
know."

"I haven't been there before. I'm on assignment. Banking, you remember. Do you?" Great eagerness that she
should.

She nodded and said, "They'll tell you at the bank. I
think there's an American club. Forgive me, I can see I'm
going to lose my seat if I don't go back to the compartment.
I'd better plough on with Anne Boleyn."

"Well, you know the plot," he said. "It seems too
gruesome for someone like you. You need taking care of."

It was definitely time to wave and go back into the
compartment. She smiled at him through the window, just
sufficiently, and closed the sliding door, going on reading by
torchlight.

Two hours later, when she was still awake, men un-
hitched the *wagon-restaurants*. She stood in the now-empty
corridor, watching the uncoupling. The cars of claret and
smoked trout and embossed menus were dragged into a

siding, and the rest of the train went on without them. It was a village train now. Soon there would be stops at small places where goats and hens would be pushed aboard in the cheaper wooden-seated compartments. She took out a handful of French centimes and threw them upward out of the window as they moved off. Burning coals flung up from the engine made the coins glitter like firework sparks before the arc of their fall.

2

◆

CATHERINE'S house—very
much hers, not her husband's—was on the banks of the
Bosphorus. It was a magnificent old place of cupolas and
arches, built in the early eighteenth century of planks painted
a pure, lucid blue, even more beautiful after centuries of
fading in the sun. Big windows opening onto terraces on two
of the floors looked across the straits. Reflections from the
water flashed on the ceilings like darting neon fish. Françoise,
her maid, carried her luggage into the house. Catherine sat
down for a moment on an iron seat to look at the place,
aware that she was being watched. There were cats staring at
her from the fence, the familiar cats that were everywhere in
Istanbul, but the peering she was alert to was a human's. She
caught a pair of brown eyes watching above the fence. As
soon as their gazes met, he declared himself and came to her
with a bundle of mail. It was the garden boy, Sukru, who
doubled as anyone's letter courier. She spoke to him in
Turkish. His thumbprints were all over the backs of the
envelopes, but she simply smiled and took the pile from him
and found some piastres for his tip, a regular amount gravely
regarded by both as his salary. Given such accord, it seemed
apt to open the letters in front of him. They were all in
French, Italian, or English; one from a musicologist that she

had been waiting for. Nothing for the boy to trade in even if he were hoping to be a spy. He seemed perfectly explicable as any other of the swarming Istanbul urchins living off their wits with some bravado. They were part of the citizenry: child professionals in an oral heritage, practicing a trade as old as diplomacy. These information attachés, uneducated except by the schooling of Istanbul's bequest of street talk, had learned to keep their ears alert to the throwaways of others in the well-founded hope that such things would be quickly salable to their more frightened elders.

Sukru's nature was familiar enough for her to know that his insistent watching of the envelopes' being opened was no more than insatiable curiosity without function. "I kept them faithfully for you as they arrived," he said proudly. "The mails are very unreliable because of the War."

"We're still at peace, Sukru."

"But preparations everywhere," he said, lowering his voice enough to provoke the suspicion proper to his adulthood, his man-of-the-worldliness.

"You're quite right, of course." She wondered whether the grown-up professionalism he donned would stand the strain of being warned to wash his hands before he attempted to make a career of steaming open letters for bribes in wartime.

"The outbreak must come any day now," he said eagerly. It seemed crushing not to be as exhilarated as he was. She shook his right hand, dirty as it was, and went into the house past a statue that she was fond of. It lay on its side in deep grass, undisturbed since it had been knocked off its pedestal many a century ago. The door was open, Françoise waiting with a pretty hand-painted bowl of water and a towel. There were rose leaves in the water. Françoise was crying because she had a German fiancé. Catherine asked whether she had news of him, whether she needed to leave for Germany while she could.

"I have decided to stay, if madame will trust me."

"Oh, Françoise, what days."

"Monsieur is in Paris still?"

"He'll be in Ankara in a week or less." Catherine put her arm round Françoise's shoulder. "Wonderful that you want to stay here. Fixed points. A center of gravity."

Françoise nodded and Catherine went into the drawing room to take the dust sheets off her harpsichord and clavichord. Not that there was dust in Istanbul, but Françoise was in the habit of covering the instruments when madame was away, as though she were drawing curtains across the bedroom windows of a delicate small child needing sleep in the daytime. Portraits of fiercely mustachioed generals of the Ottoman Empire hung on the walls. Brown eyes on the alert, bodies braced for a cavalry charge. Catherine tried the instruments and started to tune them.

In another part of Istanbul, the commercial district of banks and offices, contradicted by minarets and old buildings sometimes providing props and crutches for modern ones, an assistant to the vice president of Thomas's bank was showing him over a fake Mediterranean villa on a cliff overlooking the Bosphorus. To Thomas's mind there was too much bowing and scraping from the man, along with an obduracy he could not put his finger on. But let it go.

"This is the bank's villa? My forerunner's?"

"Yes," said the vice presidential assistant.

"One pays rent, though?"

The man from the bank bowed, expressing contempt.

"It goes to the bank, this rent?"

"One imagines."

"How much?"

"A matter for yourself to discuss."

"Everything is discussion here." Thomas controlled himself, and said of an uncomprehending Oriental manservant, "Does he come with the place?"

The vice presidential assistant looked impatient. "There is no charge. You will require him to do all your biddings."

"In America we hate elitism," said Thomas.

"In Istanbul you would perhaps not yet have knowledge of laundries," said the vice presidential assistant.

The Chinese servant closed the French doors against the sound of traffic.

Thomas said to the vice presidential assistant, "But I like the traffic. It makes me think of Wall Street."

"A flavorsome name. Wall Street. We have many ancient walls here that you will be shown."

"In fact, I like the traffic better than the house, which is pretty shoddy." Thomas knocked on the thin walls and looked at the top of them, which failed by an eighth of an inch of jerry-building to meet the ceiling.

The vice presidential assistant shrugged. "Builders for the modern taste. It is not the Turkish way, of course."

"This silence," said Thomas, reopening the windows to show a little authority, "it isn't silence, it's stagnation. Will the bank refurnish?" He sat on the bed. "I shall need an orthopedic bed. I need to keep my back in shape for squash."

"But this is a big bed of the finest quality."

"All the same, it will have to be changed," said Thomas.

Aware that the vice presidential assistant was despising him for foreign tiresomeness, he again asserted himself and said, "Can one swim in the Bosphorus? It smells of germs."

The vice presidential assistant slammed a volley. "My family swims each day at dusk in private waters drawn from the famous straits."

"The city of pleasure," said Thomas.

"The overpopulated waters are not considered salubrious. Your manservant swims in them, however."

Thomas said to the bank's man, shouting in the will to win this game of idle condescensions, "So your favored family isn't stricken with the plague because your waters are private? I suppose the nobler antibodies are quicker to build up."

The vice presidential assistant said, "There is a swift immunity to the Bosphorus."

The manservant bowed politely, understanding nothing.

Feeling entirely at a disadvantage, Thomas shook hands with the vice presidential assistant and said that he would be glad if the manservant could provide him with service every day at a fee to be decided.

"He works round the clock. He has his quarters here," said the vice presidential assistant.

Thomas was too tired to deal with the situation, too tired to ask about washing machines or bacon and eggs or whether the manservant was reliable at keeping to hours. He asked the bank's man if he could get an alarm call.

"Feel no alarm. There is no emergency. Everything will be taken care of to your satisfaction."

An end, please. Eventually the man left. Thomas stepped out onto his terrace and looked at the narrow old pathways of steps in a hilly district where a big house of faded blue planking stood out in a weedy garden.

On September the third he was in the American bank as usual. He had heard the news of

England declaring war on Germany and went to work at once on its effect on currencies. The exchange rates were moving on the board too fast for the lethargic bank boys to keep up with the changes needed in the chalked figures. He took to doing calculations on paper and exchanging news with his compatriots of what they could pick up from shortwave radios broadcasting figures from Wall Street and the City of London. Much about gas masks, air raid warnings, evacuation preparations. Not enough financial news, though the effect of the crisis could be guessed at in some currencies. Professionals had to start thinking in black market rates, anathema to them but insisted on by scores of clients blocking communications. Big investors were calling at all hours through Wall Street. Apt to think himself a failure if he stopped for breath, he took refuge in histrionics and shouted to the telephone operator that the lines to New York were medieval. Understanding no insult in that, she responded with courtliness.

Thomas looked up from his pile of papers and suddenly saw Catherine.

"How long have you been here?"

"Three or four minutes. You were busy."

"We met on the train," he said laboriously.

"Yes," she said. Her clothes were crisply ironed and he suppressed a longing to ask her advice about a laundry. Under his desk, he tried to press a pleat into the legs of his trousers between his fingers. "You had your hair set," he said instead.

"Yesterday the hairdresser was almost empty," she said. "And then I passed by today and the place was packed. I thought it would be closed on a day like this."

"Why?"

She wondered if he were serious.

"Is it a Muslim holiday?" he said.

"The declaration of war. I suppose one finds it comforting to do something usual."

"So you came to a bank. That's usual for me, but I shouldn't think it's particularly calming for you?" Thomas looked questioning.

"I need to cash some traveler's checks. My husband usually sends someone. Before we do business—before I ask you about business—" She broke off as a Turkish employee brought her a copper beaker of coffee. For Thomas, with a faint look of distaste, he brought a cup of boiling water. Thomas drew open his desk drawer and pulled out some sugar and a tin of American dehydrated coffee. "And some cream from the refrigerator," he said to the coffee provider.

The provider, who knew Catherine well, bowed and said in Turkish, "Mr. Drake prefers mud coffee, madame."

"What was he saying?" said Thomas when the man had glided away for the cream.

"That you prefer what he calls mud coffee."

"It's this Turkish coffee that I'd call mud coffee. It's like soil. I hate to think of the general state of the mileage of Turkish intestines. They drink it all day."

"I've loved it ever since I was ten. I had it first at a Turkish restaurant in London where I used to be taken by my grandmother. She had a passion for Turkish coffee. She couldn't bear French coffee because of the chicory."

"She can't have been very happy that you married a Frenchman."

"Not enough to prevent her from coming to the wedding."

"Well," said Thomas, trying bravado, "then it's me that's not happy." She smiled. "Did we ever go into the question of squash?" he said.

"You did."

"Would you like to play tonight?"

On September the third? she thought. "I'm afraid I've got a reception to go to. It's called putting a face on things."

"What's happening to the franc?" Thomas asked her, though why expect her to know. "The bank can't get Paris on the radio. You probably can." Today he felt that she could probably do anything, including, he thought, so magically managing to find him at the place where he worked.

"I've no idea," she said. "Apart from the traveler's checks, I came in to exchange a Turkish check for three people's wages. I want to pay them in dollars. They're going to have a long haul and dollars will be worth a mint. My own French bank hasn't any left. With a laissez-passer I thought even a strange American bank would honor a check for me."

"You're likely to lose on the exchange. The piastre's losing ground every minute against the dollar." He looked at her and said for decisiveness, "It's rather complicated to explain. Anyway, there's little enough involved," when he had inspected the check. He called a teller, but no one came. Catherine caught a glimpse of a bill in some currency passing from a hard-faced woman waiting at the counter to a boy who could possibly be Sukru. Over in a flash. A man in the background was speaking rapidly in German about a credit note. About the exactness of the exchange. Thomas watched, and said to Catherine, "Well, he got service. The tellers have been saying to me for hours that I'm breaking into their lunch hour. Lunch *hour*, they call it. It lasts three."

Catherine said, "They're neutral. Also kind. They wouldn't shout at a German client on September the third."

Thomas said, after a pause, "This war will be over by Christmas."

"Yes, one says that, doesn't one," said Catherine. "Your family must be concerned that you're here."

"The land of *luxe et volupté*. As the tellers are off, shall we have lunch? There's a Yugoslavian restaurant that looked promising."

*T*hey went across the Galata Bridge. Thomas was thunderstruck by the sight of Istanbul and looked it. The domes and minarets, the brilliant purpled blues that shone when the sun was on them like stained glass more beautiful than any he had ever seen, the vaulted fifteenth-century shops, the winding streets and steps of old Stamboul, the imperial city divided from the port quarter by the crook of water called the Golden Horn. The city was indeed gilded, often with the gold of Byzantium. He was not used to anything that so encompassed the ramshackle and the magnificent, and made the city as a whole majestic.

"Yes," said Catherine, watching his face. "I never get used to it either." She told him about the seven hills of Istanbul. "Ex-Constantinople, ex-Byzantium. It's the only city in the world which stands on two continents. That's the main part"—pointing—"the southeastern tip of Europe. The Bosphorus divides it from the Asian suburbs."

Thomas caught sight of a cobbler sitting grinning in a barrel by the waterside. "Who's that?" he said.

"A cobbler in a barrel."

"Working in a barrel?"

"Living and working in a barrel."

"Who owns those houses?" he said, pointing to old wooden mansions in colors faded by centuries of sun.

"People like me," she said.

"You actually have one of those?"

"Yes."

"Straight on to the water?"

"Well, no one's drowned yet."

21

"There's space between the houses. But no gardens, just weeds."

"The gardens are at the back. Not gardens in any model-apartment sense. This isn't a place that writers of Manhattan city-garden books would approve of. The Turkish don't need to *use* space. Utilitarianism hasn't hit Istanbul. There's enough space to go round. The gardens just happen. They grow wild."

Thomas said, "Civilization running to seed. But still, it's stunning."

Catherine looked at him. "That's not so contradictory, is it?"

"I've just never seen anything like it."

"There is nowhere like it. I don't know—maybe Kiev—but I doubt it. Shall we have some raki before lunch?"

"Where?"

"On the lower bit of the bridge there are a lot of cafés. One could have a little something local in a glass, and look at the Sea of Marmara meeting the Golden Horn."

Or I could look at you, he thought. They had their glasses of raki, lingered, and then started again for the Yugoslavian restaurant. They talked on the way about the innumerable wild cats in Istanbul. "Watching you everywhere you go," said Thomas.

"Witnesses, not voyeurs, though," said Catherine, putting a hand on his arm. And then, quietly, as the restaurant came in sight, "I'm afraid the German plan of occupation will have Yugoslavia high on the list."

"Will we be unwelcome at lunch?"

"A comfort, if anything. We're all in this. Neutrality's impossible for any of us except on paper. It's a wonder there's a Yugoslavian restaurant here at all."

"Why?"

"Yugoslavia was under Turkish rule for rather a long time."

"But that was the Ottoman Empire," said Thomas. She turned her blaze of a smile to him and said, "You do have a gift for bringing history to heel."

3

♦

WHEN Paris fell, Catherine asked Thomas to her house for comfort instead of always lunching out. They sat on the terrace of her bedroom. It was June, but suddenly a chill day. They had rugs over their knees, and at noon Catherine's maid had brought them mugs of delicate chicken broth.

"It's as if we're on board ship," said Catherine.

"Because of the Bosphorus?"

"And the bouillon, and our sitting here with rugs as if we were on a boat deck."

"Bouillon."

"The broth they bring you on ships for elevenses, as if one didn't have anything to do but eat all day on liners. Peacetime liners, that is." She looked at the packed refugee ships.

"I'd like to show you the Great Lakes. I'd like to show you Mark Twain's riverboats. Wouldn't your husband mind my being here?"

"Why should he?"

"It's rather intimate." He sipped some broth. "Sitting about in the daytime."

"You sound guilty about enjoying it. When I was a girl in France I had an English nanny who said it was a sin to read a novel in the morning."

"Do you think I'm not motivated?" Thomas looked greatly concerned. "This job really matters to me. The war's making it difficult. I keep sending memos to Wall Street but they don't seem to understand that the War's preoccupying everyone here. They tell me Turkey's neutral so what's all this about the War affecting Istanbul? You wouldn't think you'd have to explain about Turkey's strategic importance. The Balkans. Air bases." He sighed, the sigh of a child explaining the self-evident to the grown-ups in authority. Catherine thought suddenly of a story she particularly liked of a nine-year-old banished to bed, saying at the top of the stairs to the roomful of adults below, "And good-night to all my critics." Her friend seemed to suspect himself of being an innocent surrounded by critics in this strange continent.

"You're Madame de Rochefauld," he said insistently. "Where *is* the monsieur of the place?"

"Just arrived in Ankara from Paris. His name's Jean-Pierre," she said. "You'll meet him one day. He and I have what I think the women's magazines politely call separate lives." She thought about him with long fondness and said, "Mentally separate, mostly. Not emotionally, though other people seem to think he's rigorous and cold. He's actually a romantic man."

"He's in the foreign service?"

"He has a rather special function. It's not a titular role. He happens to be an authority on Turkish history."

"Is he older than you?"

"Yes. By the usual European amount, I suppose."

"Then how does he keep in shape?"

"What?"

"Physically, how does he cope with the age difference?"

"It's got more to do with his mind. That's where his energy comes from, I think."

"So his exercise is really intellectual."

"He's just intensely interested."

"And of course he plays chess."

Catherine saw him looking back at the chessboard laid out on the floor of a huge room behind him. It was a marble board, with ancient carved chessmen. "Yes, and draughts. That's the strategic aspect of his mind," she said.

"Who does he play against?"

"Me."

"So you've got it too. This aspect of mind."

"Not up to his."

"I haven't got it at all. I suppose there isn't any more broth?" He turned round in his deck chair to look at her. "He sounds *very* motivated."

That word again. He clearly felt he was failing at something. "What is it?" she said.

He wondered if he could touch her, and did, using his fingers as a comb to run through her hair. She bent her head back. "Tell me," she said.

"I've suddenly found I can't keep figures in my head. Currency conversions. I have to write them down. I've never had to before. My memory for calculating's turned to pure flab."

"Dear friend, you're the only man I've ever known who talked about the money market as if it were morning exercises."

"Well, it is. Up at dawn for deep breathing about the dollar and cut down on fats for the peso. Damn the peso. I like it here." And then, "Is 'friend' all I am?"

"It's a lot," she said.

He went on playing with her hair and said, "You called this house ramshackle but it's more like living in the Plaza. The Plaza Hotel."

She made a face on behalf of her house.

Regain ground. He tried. "A Byzantine Plaza, I meant. Or Ottoman Empire Plaza. A real estate agent wouldn't know how to begin."

" 'Unique run-down elegance.' "

"I didn't mean to sound callow. I'm just amazed always by this city. Is it thriving after Ataturk?"

"Nearly all Europe is poorly now because of the War. Neutral Turkey has been badly off for decades. Now it's up for barter and valued. The wheelers-and-dealers and voyeurs are everywhere."

"There are two cats looking at you from the balcony."

Catherine said, after identifying them, "They're familiars."

"Didn't ancient witches have familiars?"

"Or ghosts? I'm not up on things like that."

"Shall we go for a swim, as I'm still not at the bank? How long do siestas take?"

She laughed and said, "It would depend on the siesta taker, wouldn't it? If you mean the bank tellers, you said three hours."

He looked at his watch and said, "Then we've got twenty-five minutes."

"It will be pretty cold."

"But it's seventy-two degrees."

"There's a wind from somewhere."

He wet his right index finger and held it up and said, "I don't feel it."

"A wind howling in my guts. The War, I expect. Does your watch tell the temperature, too?"

"It tells me the time in Paris, New York, London, Berlin, Tokyo, the year, the altitude, and the compass bearing. And of course the time here." The time with you, which runs out faster than a man should have to bear. "And, as you say, the temperature." He stood and looked poised to dive from the balcony, clothes and all. Away with caution in this new land.

"Does it tell your temperature, too? Because there probably are the germs you suspect in the Bosphorus and you won't have built up antibodies." She stretched back still further and seemed to expect no answer.

"You do use silences," he said. "I do, of course, too. Financiers do. To find out what a client really wants." He sat down again as an assertion and said, "It could turn out to be one of things we have in common." He paused.

"So go on," she said, holding his hand.

"Two things," he said, earnest in effort. "I'm in love with you. With you in particular. But what I suppose I'd hoped to find in the Middle East was an older woman to love. That's the second thing on my mind. I'd expected to fall in love with an experienced woman."

"I should think I'm older enough than you are to qualify," she said as soberly as she could. "I'm thirty-one at least, nearly thirty-two. And you must be twenty-eight because you said you only had twelve years of high prowess to go in finance before the fatal age of forty. You said it was also the fatal age of the onset of decline for philosophers and higher mathematicians, and even worse for squash players."

"Are you hurt by my saying 'older woman'?"

She looked at him with the solemnity he seemed to want and then saw that he didn't at all. "What was the *real* second thing?"

Thomas walked about. He looked at his watch without taking in anything but the movement of it.

"When I first came here I was very thrown because I was used to regular office hours," he said.

"Routine."

"Discipline."

"Not the same thing, is it?" said Catherine. "You can be disciplined any hour of the day or night, can't you?"

"Doing what?"

"Nothing. Anything."

"This erratic life doesn't suit me professionally. I don't function."

Catherine said softly, "Oh, that word." Pause. "Thomas, you do. You pay heed, you change things. What more?"

Thomas said, "I can't manage without working hours at a long stretch. Business is all out of whack. Short bouts of speculation and then total paralysis of capital. Reluctance to invest because of some baseless fear of the future."

"Baseless? It would be real fear, wouldn't it? The War."

"I seem to be cashing a tremendous number of traveler's checks for visitors who are panicking the market."

Catherine said, getting up, "Look at the river. Those aren't visitors you're seeing. Those are refugees. There's another shipload coming in."

"How can you tell they're refugees?"

"I can hear them."

"I can't."

"I'm more used to silence than you, probably."

Thomas sat down beside her and twisted her wedding ring. "I'm happy, more happy than I've ever been, but I don't feel right. I don't even like my glasses." He took them off. "They've got square rims." He had a way sometimes of looking at his possessions as if they had simply happened to him.

Catherine said, "Why don't you get some with round rims, then? They're cheap enough here for people with dollars."

"They're prescription glasses. I'm not sure that I'd trust a Turkish oculist. Not yet."

"I know one who makes up Jean-Pierre's prescriptions for him."

Thomas was incensed. "Catherine! Jean-Pierre's oculist? Are you suggesting my going to your husband's oculist?"

He walked round and round the balcony, long arms swinging a little forward as if he were a bear caged in a cliché about love. "It should be Jean-Pierre who's jealous, not me."

"Don't be guilty. You're not taking anything away from him." She held his hand again and lifted her head to feel the breeze, getting her hair over her face and blowing it away as she spoke. "Do you truly like it here?"

"So much that I can't leave. It's as if we were completely surrounded by water and I can't even swim."

"But you can. All you have to do is take your time."

"Do you take your time?"

"You'd know that better than I do," she said.

"You just obey your nature, don't you? Or even only your mood."

She looked at him carefully. "How try to explain people?"

They moved downstairs, looking up at the glass dome over the top staircase. Thomas said, "Byzantine?"

"Style of. It would be called a cupola, I suppose. It makes me think of St. Paul's. Or the follies of the Brighton Pavilion. Have you ever been to Brighton?"

"Your Prince Regent's place? No. Could we go very soon?"

"After Christmas," she said.

"You sound dry," he said.

She said, "It'll pass. I was whipped back into France and England."

"As if you weren't there all the time in your head."

"I just think that the War being over by Christmas isn't on the cards."

In the drawing room she found him a book on the Brighton Pavilion. He looked at the chinoiserie, the brocades, and most of all the complexity of cupolas. "It's great," he said.

"People didn't think so when it was built," she said. "Sydney Smith, who was a pamphleteer of the day, said that it looked as if the Dome of St. Paul's had come to Brighton and pupped."

He looked distressed. "I don't like caustic wit. It's very English. Or very French. I guess you're going to call that parochial of me." She shook her head. Encouraged, he said, "I just don't care for anything in funniness that's said in hidden inflection marks."

She stroked a muslin curtain that was blowing in the breeze and said, "Yes. There was a gently funny man you'd have liked very much who said that the wit he most admired was the wit that went home without drawing blood."

"Sometimes you talk more like an Englishwoman than a Frenchwoman. When you're telling me things you respond to."

"Only when I'm with you. When I'm alone with other people here I feel French."

"Because you're a wife."

"Maybe."

"Do you think in French?"

She tried to reply. "I'm not sure there's an honest answer. I don't know. It's like the old question of whether you dream in color or black and white."

"What about the way you see the War in dreams?"

"It's best if I can manage to see it in black and white, because that turns it into a newsreel that could have been

31

shot a long time ago. Meaning that it's over. Pray God that it were. 'The last just war.' "

"Did you say that?"

"Who doesn't?" There was something she needed to say to him. "Look, it's not your fault America isn't in the War yet." She leaned forward to him. "Practically everyone except Roosevelt in America seems to feel that this is a European war."

"I'm not sure I don't," he said.

She sat up on the embroidered cushions where they were lying and picked up two draughtsmen, took off his spectacles, and put the draughtsmen gently over his eyes. "I like you in round specs," she said, half closing her own eyes as if she were painting him. He suddenly looked as stilled and familiar to her as the big photographs on the wall: the family portraits in sepia of her mother as a droop-shouldered girl, her wasp-waisted aunt in her early twenties, her grandmother with loops of soft hair. Sunlight broken up by the white-painted shutters glittered onto the bright Turkish carpet with its clear blues and reds and brilliant blacks. In front of the muslin curtains, the French brocade curtains drawn back in swags were so old and brittle that they had nearly turned to paper. She must have them mended somehow, she thought, as Thomas drew her down onto the cushions and kissed her hair.

"Round spectacles?" she said.

"Done and done," he said, taking off his watch and putting it on her wrist. "I always forget how much smaller women's wrists are than men's." She opened her fingers to show him the spread of her hand. "But not necessarily the handspan," she said. She measured it against his and said, "You see?"

"It would be from playing the harpsichord. Or spinet, is it?"

"That's a harpischord, and that's a clavichord," she said, pointing.

"What's the difference?"

"I'll try to explain later," she said.

"A good deal later," he said, forgetting the bank.

It was only when he went back there, indeed much later, when everyone else had gone, that he looked at his wrist and realized he'd left the watch on hers. She had said she was going to a reception. Some Turkish official party. He hoped she was wearing the watch there, perhaps hidden under a long sleeve.

*I*n her bedroom, Catherine looked at herself in the looking glass and kept his watch on instead of her own. Some new mode, if anyone of that much curiosity wondered. People at diplomatic functions missed nothing under their absorption in keeping to trivia. On the brink of a crisis, third secretaries' wives would exchange recipes with other third secretaries' wives as long as they were *en poste* at a friendly embassy, and an eavesdropper would always be there to memorize the recipes in case they might be some vital strategic signal.

She drove herself to the Turkish reception. Handshaking. There was talk of the terrible earthquake in Asia Minor. The German second secretary's wife said, with a tinkling laugh, "Divine wrath at Turkey's abandonment of her former ally," meaning Germany in the First World War and much fishing later, as everyone knew. In an only barely permissible way in diplomacy, she was making a provocative comment with the knowledge that she was safely on neutral territory. People pretended politely that she did not mean Germany, that she did not mean anything political, that what she was saying had no political content, least of all to do with the

Turkish nonaggression pact with England and France. One did not speak politics at diplomatic gatherings.

Ann Wisner came up to Catherine and said, "Darling, am I fearfully bruised? I got under the knife just before the surgeon quit for America. Where there are more potential patients not yet thinking about munitions. He promised me the bruises would go."

"It must have hurt," was all that Catherine could think of to say.

"It was idiotic of me," said Ann. She lowered her voice and said, "There's too much talk about you, darling. Is it because of Thomas? I keep hearing his name. Does Jean-Pierre know of his existence?"

"Yes, because the driver came up from Ankara for some clothes he wanted."

"The driver you don't trust."

"It seems to me that he's—well, at least happier on his home ground."

Ann looked around her. At people valiantly pretending ease when they felt that they had no more than a finger-nail's purchase on their world's cliff-face. "Don't we all," Catherine said, reading Ann's expression. She stubbed out a Turkish cigarette and started to say, "Protocol helps," before the British naval attaché's wife found herself anchored by a dress hook to the back of the German ambassadress. It took a Turkish official ten minutes to disentangle them.

Ann Wisner murmured about the involvement that it was "nothing of a political nature—" with more than a gleam of humor.

At the same time, a tactful Scots academic in retirement was saying that he had no idea how it could have happened, considering the care taken by the Turks "for the nonce" that British and German representatives should never be in the same official room, "let alone allied by a hook fastener."

Catherine thought for a moment. About the absurdity made possible by sophistication, and about how much easier it might be to deal with aggressive intent at the Neanderthal level of throwing rocks. "I don't understand how the British naval attaché's wife was asked," she said.

"Her husband's away. The naval attaché. She's said to be rather dim," said Ann.

"I expect she found an invitation for last year and simply didn't look at the date," said Catherine. "Or took it upon herself, as you might say, to promote the Turkish sense of honor by asking for Turkish aid at a dressmaking rank, which she would rightly regard as being a lot safer than all these demands for spare parts for airplanes promised in treaties that her husband is trying to keep stitched together."

The British ambassador was in the ballroom. Catherine watched a Turkish official go up to him and lead him away. Three-quarters of an hour's absence. She came out into the corridor on the pretext of powdering her nose in private and caught a glimpse of them coming down the stairs outside the party. The British ambassador ran into the counselor of the American Embassy and grabbed his arm, changing course and coming back to the ballroom engaged in deep conversation. Everyone started now to divert their speculations about what Britain and Turkey had been discussing to speculations about an attempt by Britain to bring America into the War.

Ann said in a low voice, "What's Thomas's last name?"

Catherine thought it best to eat a stuffed vine leaf so that her reply could be mumbled. "Thomas Drake." And then, more loudly, "Oh my dear, I've made a spot on your dress." She grabbed a siphon of soda water and spurted it onto her handkerchief before going for Ann's skirt on her hands and knees, saying "Sh."

"You must so want him in the War. It must be such a gap between you."

"I think we should talk to some of the French people here."

They parted, and Catherine started to talk to an elderly French woman, famous in Paris simply as Jeanne, who had taken refuge from France's drift on grounds very much other than fear. Catherine knew Ann admired her. She was ageless, well dressed, a little like Coco Chanel, known in Paris for decades as the most eminent madam of them all. Her girls were beauties, retained by abdicated kings, housed in beautiful suites, dressed by the couture. She had been imprisoned for four months.

Catherine thought it not at all wrong to kiss her on both cheeks.

"No prison pallor," she said in English. "What did they get you for?"

"Tax."

"Forgive me, but wasn't it really to do with being against the Vichy government?"

"No. Tax authorities find politics trivial. They wanted to tax me on my earnings and I didn't think it was correct. My earnings as a procuress. Why should I give a bad name to the State? I love France. There is no reason why I should drag the name of France in the dirt. They consider my profession dirt, so my position is impossible. If my business had been recognized as legal, believe me, I would gladly have paid. I am an honest woman."

Catherine nodded, stupefied. Only in France.

"As to Pétain, though," said Jeanne with dignity, "I do feel him to be wrong. Pétain is in association with the Führer. For myself, I am for de Gaulle."

"They spring from the same soil. They both went to Saint-Cyr."

"Everyone knows that in the old days de Gaulle said, 'Pétain is a great man,' and that now he says, 'He was a great man.' You're for Pétain?"

"We're in the diplomatic service."

Jeanne nodded. "But you yourself?"

"My husband serves France's government."

Jeanne laughed.

"What is it?"

"Here I am, notoriously making a packet out of a notion that women are men's playthings without minds of their own. But I am not outside society for that. I am outside it because the economy decides to include me. Society in the person of tax collectors, denying my very sober respect for the integrity of France, imprisons me for not paying tax on, as they see it, an illegal income. This is ignoble. If their argument was that I made women serfs, then I would respect them, though they would be wrong. It is they who are the serfs, the serfs of money. Naturally I believe in women's independence of thought. Yet when I express my opinions people don't take me to be serious. And now I find that, when I ask you about *your* opinions, you quite possibly find yourself with the same anomaly to deal with because your husband is in the diplomatic service. The world thus demotes you to being a good harnessed wife in agreement with the official form of French loyalty as upheld by Pétain, which is fascism. You would do better to declare for de Gaulle. Then people with their childish worldliness would think the earth of you because they would take you to be acting a pretense so as to protect a Nazi lover."

"Do you think that?"

"I shall if you want me to," Jeanne said seriously, deciding to ignore the fact that a waiter was listening too intently for comfort. If one censored oneself for eaves-droppers' sakes, one could feel very guilty indeed.

"Where has your mind wandered to?" said Jeanne, who had not taken her eyes off Catherine.

"I'd just remembered a bugged bath plug we found in the embassy."

"Cockroaches?"

"No, bugged as in wiretap."

"To be expected," said Jeanne.

"Yes, Jean-Pierre told me so too. But it stopped us talking for a while." Catherine paused.

"What stopped you just then? said Jeanne.

Catherine, because the waiter was still hovering, kept the bath plug firmly in mind and said more loudly than usual, "I was trying to remember the Turkish for cockroaches. If indeed Turkey has cockroaches." She smiled and said "Merci" at some caviar canapés that the waiter pressed on her as his permitted form of eavesdropping, and deflected him by saying in Turkish, "I beg your pardon. I intended *merci* in the French sense of no thank-you." The waiter was obliged to go away.

Jeanne said, "And now where were we."

"Pétain, say."

"Directly continuing from waiters, cockroaches, my profession, and your position." Jeanne was perhaps the most serious person in the room, thought Catherine.

"Pétain did the right thing by somehow getting round our Reynaud of the fighting spirit so that Paris could be declared an open city to Hitler," Catherine tried out. "At least we were spared heroics."

Jeanne spat. "I'm not spitting at what you say, but because you're a terrible actress."

"I'm not acting."

"For a living bath plug," Jeanne said, nodding toward the waiter, who had been called further away but seemed to be rounding back.

Catherine drove on. "On May the twenty-eighth Pétain wisely said to de Gaulle, 'We must capitulate. What you say to the country is stupid and childish. I'm old and experienced and I know that England is lost. The War is finished.' "

Jeanne looked at her, amused, and said, "You say that as if Pétain had convinced you, but I don't believe you for a minute because you say it with the will of Wellington. I want to give you acting lessons. It's quite vital. We will call them lessons in elocution. And perhaps we should talk about history. In my experience people are pro-Vichy or anti-Vichy largely according to whether they thought that in the last Great War Pétain had been the hero of Verdun or defeatist."

"The old boy has seen something like a hundred and seven governments in his time and he was born at the end of the Crimean War. He may be right."

"The acting is improving."

"Pétain may be an old despot, but at least he comes from a continent crowded with frontiers."

"Unlike your American. You think I don't hear about him, and the speculation about your views that arises from your separation from your Catholic Vichy husband, and safeguard you?" said Jeanne in a low voice. And then, so as to be heard, "I like Pétain's talkativeness about his troubles with his garden."

"Go on," said Catherine, an eye on the waiter.

"You see, there it is, the anomaly again," said Jeanne. "The atrocious dictator who's also a winning old fusspot. He thought he was the glory of France and there he is grumbling about his garden boy. He thinks the gardener's a spendthrift about fertilizers."

Catherine said her good-byes and left to walk home up and down the paths of old steps that made the thoroughfares. The Golden Horn spread like an index finger into the Bosphorus. Outside the Byzantine walls of the old city, fortune-tellers were telling the future by lantern light. Not to the usual tourists, but to the refugees who had who knows what future. The little shops curtained with strings of beads were still open along the steep pathways. Leather shops, craft shops, cobblers, fabric sellers, bookshops, herb sellers. She stopped abruptly to look into a bookshop window. What she had thought to be the echo of her own footsteps halted a fraction too late. She turned around and smiled and raised her hand in recognition of the waiter. He wore an uncomfortable-looking overcoat over his uniform, with the collar turned up in a void attempt to cover his black tie. She went back to him.

He might shoot her. But he might also shoot her if she went on, and he had nothing whatever in the way of evidence against her. She made a "May I?" gesture with her eyebrows and undid his black tie, folded it to be put into his coat pocket, and turned up the collar of his shirt with the top button undone. Embarrassment at her housemaid's role paralyzed him and empowered her to smile again swiftly, say "There," as to a child, and turn away again to walk on. One doesn't often get away with such chances, she said to herself, and bravado isn't courage.

4

♦

CATHERINE was asked to go on a duck shoot. The German ambassador, no ready Nazi, was on a visit to Istanbul, while his staff moved him from the German Embassy into the Czech Legation. He knew Catherine well enough to say when he called on her, "The staff is an exhausting lot of Heil-Hitlerites now. You've seen Hindenburg's portrait in the embassy, but I'm inclined to refrain from hanging a portrait of the Führer for the moment. The absence of it makes negotiations more tranquil. When the staff is around, one's own arms and legs get stiff by proxy before the mind has had a chance. Talking of goose-stepping—though I see you blink at the Freudian flight of ideas of a phrase which at least keeps us to birds and will not allow us to skelter off into talk of the Austrian Anschluss—I am, as you know, totally crazy about duck shooting. And now that we're in Istanbul I propose to take the chance. Tomorrow. In Ankara we have always had a problem with too much flat land and no bushes and hedges for us to hide in, but Istanbul is another kettle of fish and I'm keen to show you. I'm asking the Italian and Bulgarian attachés to join us. And any one else keen on the sport you might like to ask. You may be the only woman, Catherine." He kissed her hand and went back to his car.

"Shooting Turkish ducks is not as easy as it might seem," she said later to Thomas, who turned out to have been asked. "The German ambassador is embracing Istanbul because it has all the possible hides and camouflage that Ankara hasn't."

"It will mean another day of playing hooky from work," he said in a neutral voice.

She wondered if he loathed any blood sport and wouldn't have blamed him. She said, "I think I'd be a vegetarian if I faced the point. I'm not going to do any shooting at all, I've decided. Don't join in the massacre if you don't want to. It's the Ambassador's day, anyway. And think how bracingly early we'll be getting up. Wall Street time. You might drop a few memos to Wall Street impressing them with your dawn rise and the distinguished company."

"To instill the idea of diligence," said Thomas, feeling a long way away from banking.

She kissed him. "Wear woolen trousers and heavy shoes, I should."

Thomas said, "You seem to take a dim view of blue denims."

"Darling, I often wear them myself when we're alone. Just not in front of Françoise."

"As if we ever knew when we were in front of Françoise. She's forever coming and going."

"She always knocks."

"And you always say come in. Also your blue denims are pale lilac."

"I'll look like a dowager tomorrow, I promise. Long tweed skirt, cardigans, boots. You'll see."

He did, come the next dawn, and felt more rapt by her than ever. Who would have thought to see Catherine in three layers of hand-knitted white cardigans with pockets sagging to her knees. "This one belonged to my great-aunt," she said when he picked her up at four in the morning. "She wore it to go out for the salt."

"Badly off?"

"Rich as Croesus. My great-uncle bought sea salt by the boulder and kept it in a potting shed. She hacked it with an ax."

"In America we have quite a lot of pickax murders," he said with dignity.

She held his hand and gave him a map. It was a long drive. When they arrived, the German ambassador was seeing to the unloading of four domesticated ducks borrowed from the Ankara Zoo and brought up by local train. Each duck had been trussed and fitted with a long string lead. The wild ducks on the lake, alert to the hostile human busyings, were flying off in scores.

"Now we shall throw our four tame ducks into the water as decoys," said the German ambassador happily. "And holding on to the leads carefully, I shall dig a hide for myself and my gun, and you as my guests will camouflage yourselves with branches and brambles especially flown in from Ankara." It was comforting to Catherine that the German ambassador, the very emissary of the Führer himself, had somehow totally forgotten the native camouflage of Istanbul that he had explained to be the whole reason for the intricate importation of the zoo ducks from Ankara. His mistake had exasperated his zealously efficient staff. They had a war on their minds, they said, not a duck shoot. Out of the blue, they had been ordered to make advisory overnight calls to the guests to prepare for costuming in imported foliage that would be available at dawn at the lake. There being, as the Ambassador had said, a great shortage of foliage around Ankara, the staff had irritably ransacked a larger neighborhood for a supply of reasonable leafery. This had then been flown by special plane to Istanbul, ignoring the mass of it locally rampant. Foreign powers routinely listening in to telephone calls were alert to the obviously coded messages.

Six people, Catherine and Thomas included, swathed themselves in the now limp camouflage. Catherine murmured something about Birnam Wood to Thomas, who replied that Dunsinane would be a good name for the British ambassador.

"Unfortunately absent because he is at war," whispered Catherine.

"Yes, one forgets," said Thomas, in his first moment of convivial dryness that day. They held hands, and Thomas protected the gesture with a piece of rosebush. Catherine said, "In the bastard English that the Académie is trying to keep out of French—the efforts continue unabated, forget the War—shaking hands is called 'le shake-hand.' Shall we try to find ourselves a ditch somewhere? Skedaddle if we're going to canoodle?"

"What?"

"I think I'd slipped into P. G. Wodehouse's mind."

"That's what I thought."

He paused.

"What now?" said Catherine.

"I was thinking of how on earth Bertie Wooster could have fallen for Madeleine considering she said the stars were God's daisy chain. Talking of bards, Birnam Wood shouldn't move, should it, or who knows what omens would come true?"

Suddenly two shots rang out. They were not from the German ambassador's gun. Catherine saw him scrambling out of the hide, covered with the vegetation sent up by his

Residence and gesturing dramatically. The wild ducks were indeed fluttering about in fascination with the placidity of the decoys, but it was the tame ones from the zoo who had been shot at, and the shots had not been fired by anyone in the party. Two figures were disappearing over a hillock.

"Poachers!" said the German ambassador. He started to run after them, and then Thomas and the Embassy driver ran after him. Thomas put a hand on his arm. Catherine saw them speaking rapidly, and the German ambassador using his binoculars, and then clapping Thomas on the back and asking his driver to open some thermoses. When the German ambassador came back, he was bleeding from behind the ear. Thomas was calling for a first aid kit, not the sort of thing that had occurred to the Embassy staff in Ankara to send as part of the luggage of trussed ducks.

"Our friend recognized the poachers," said the ambassador. "Tell them."

"The American and the Russian ambassadors," said Thomas.

"It is rather a diplomatic crisis," an attaché from the Swiss Embassy said with awe.

"For my part, and it would only be I who would be sending them, there will be no cables about this," said the German ambassador. "It is not a question of representatives of great powers firing on Hitler's representatives. It is because they were firing at *sitting ducks*. This is my entire complaint. It is not a cause for war. Later on—"

"—After some next Christmas—" said Thomas, with a dryness.

"—I shall see to it that something is published. I shall write my memoirs and perhaps one of you will make sure that it reaches French ears. The French feel very strongly about sitting ducks. It is not a matter of Vichy or de Gaulle here. France is as one in its position on sitting ducks."

"And in the meantime I really would like to get you some iodine," said Thomas. "I have some at the bank. You'll see Catherine home?"

"I'll come with you," said Catherine.

The German ambassador said, laughing only a little, that such efficiency as keeping iodine at the ready in a bank deserved a cable to Berlin in itself, warning of American efficiency if Roosevelt were ever to bring his country into the War. This might have made Thomas very angry, if he had heard; Catherine took it in, and felt angered on his behalf, though she behaved like a good wife of Vichy and shook hands before speeding off to the car.

5

♦

On their way back from the duck shoot, Operation Iodine achieved, Catherine thought of dropping Thomas at the bank and then told him she had seen something perturbing in the little bookshop when she had caught the waiter trailing her.

"It's a German booklet that shouldn't be there. I want to know what you think," she said. "Though I'd be making you late."

He paused, wanted to say, "The hell with it," and then said, "Could it be at lunchtime?"

"Come to my house by some detour. Everyone's being followed."

"They know you," said Thomas with a bite in his voice. "They don't know me."

"Don't you believe it," she said.

He came to the house at twelve-thirty and said to Sukru the garden boy, "Can't you put that statue back on its pedestal?" The garden boy bowed his head and smiled, with no comprehension. Catherine, in a pale orange jersey dress and a long white scarf, overheard Thomas and waited till they were outside the gate. "Sukru doesn't speak much English," she said.

"Then I'll do it. It's begun to look sloppy, lying about."

47

"It's not a coat that should be on a hanger. I like it like that. And I doubt if the pedestal's the original one anyway. I think it may once have been a sundial. It wouldn't carry the weight."

"Well, I suppose it goes with the unmown lawn."

"It was never a lawn. It's just grass," she said. She had started to say they should halt this mock-married squabble when she realized that there was something larger on his mind.

"So what's in the bazaar?" he said.

"Come on," she said, taking his arm. "All's well, considering."

"Considering what?"

"The War. What else?"

"So that's the concern. Let it go, darling. You're in the War as you, willy-nilly. You're hardly a neutral man."

They fell into a silence with one another and the testiness drained away. The two of them strolled quietly along the little streets of bead-curtained shops. From the basements, halfway below street level, there was the blare of a hundred radios playing. Once or twice she picked up news bulletins in English. Much more than shoe mending or craft work was going on behind those beaded curtains. She parted one set and saw a whispered conference that turned back into the selling of some gems as soon as she was glimpsed. She stepped back quickly with a gesture of apology about having mistaken the shop and took Thomas onward.

"We'd better look in a good many windows as we go," she said.

He nodded and strode a little ahead of her.

They came to the bookshop and she grasped his arm, pointing at some art books and saying in a low voice, "The booklet in the middle, half-hidden under the book on

48

Titian." It was an official booklet published by the German Military High Command.

"Now we'll go and have lunch," he said. "I don't get the nuance but we'd better make tracks."

"I've got a tray ready. I've given Françoise the day off."

Back in the house by the Bosphorus she said, "I think we've stumbled on a colossal blunder. I think that booklet's the one issued to German troops before they invaded Norway and Holland and France and Yugoslavia. The phrase book for the master race that copes with the commonplace events in the average occupying Nazi's day. In every language. 'For not wearing the Star of David you will be shot,' 'We are taking you to a labor camp,' 'I need a reliable dentist.' You know the sort of thing."

"I've never heard you like this."

"The bootjack doesn't often slip on a banana skin. It's terrible, it's farcical, but I'm pretty sure that phrase book's part of a set that's come to Turkey by mistake. Nazi heads are going to roll. Does it mean that Turkey's next on the list, or is it one of those things that are inexcusably excused as human fallibility?"

Thomas looked longingly at the tray set out before them on the floor but left quickly, saying simply that he'd be back. In half an hour he was.

"A hundred were issued by mistake. I've bought the ninety-three that were left."

"How did you find out?"

"I went in looking as irrevocably American as usual and paid the black market rate for the things as tourist souvenirs." She heard the wounded sarcasm and minded. "And then greased a few more palms and wrote a note to the German ambassador thanking him for the duck shoot and telling him that seven copies were somewhere at large and did he want to get in touch with me at the bank. Where, of course, I'm not."

"You'd better be. Be serious, to let him seem to unburden you by being lighthearted in case that's the way he needs to play it."

Thomas looked at her carefully, as he always did. "Yes, I see. I always thought drawing-room diplomacy wasn't a phrase for nothing. It's played as a game."

"It has to be, because the stakes in people are too high for it to be anything but a game with rules that are understood and abided by." She smiled about the two of them and said to him, "But you're bloody hungry. Just go in for a bit and leave a message for him that you were there and will be back whenever. Oh love, you're really up to your neck in things now."

"No. Only a neutral could have done it."

"That's exactly what I mean."

He ate some caviar from a teaspoon and left for the bank, thinking very little of his mission and much about Catherine. Raptness in the alert here and now; then bank business for a New York still dozing. An unvexed mixture. He felt steered.

They sat down to the tray at last. This was another drawing room, one that he had never seen before, though with the same view of the Bosphorus. There were big vivid cushions made of patterned carpet piled against the windows, brass lamps on old French furniture warped by damp but burnished carefully with beeswax. The polish left a smell of honey around the room, a trail of summer he remembered from Cape Cod and she from Provence.

"What are you thinking about?" he said.

"That it's nice that you're here, mostly. And also, I think, worrying that I may have got you into something more than you want to cope with."

"I made that choice, darling."

"You're right." She pondered.

"And what else are you thinking about?" he said.

"About the Orient Express, about seeing you on it, and about how the Nazis have commandeered the train and made it a key honor for the SS to travel on it. They've taken it over so late. A long time after every other train in occupied Europe. And the maquis keep planting the railway track with bombs and blowing themselves up along with it. The SS are cooped targets. They must be mad, to think their uniforms make them members of some sacrosanct race. Splendor before safety. Sometimes I think the Gestapo—"

"—are foolish as well as everything else," he said for her. "But you're not looking sad for them, are you?"

"Was I looking sad? I thought my face was expressionless. That's why it's a useful face."

"Darling girl, utilitarianism doesn't apply to faces."

"Sometimes."

"Anyway, you still look sad. So I'm left to guess whether you had a love in the Gestapo or a love in the Maquis who got killed in one of the underground maneuvers."

She licked a teaspoon of caviar and said, "Oh dove, that train. It's stood for so great a change in us. All the way through the nineteenth century it was something purely thought, something true, an expression of a real belief in the perfectibility of man. But now here we are, having proved ourselves to be so imperfect that the species has spawned the Nazis. The tonic fact is that a great many men and women haven't allowed themselves to be jaded." Thomas saw her in midstream, out there on her own and unreachable. He wanted to say "Some speech" to stop her, but didn't think it would even have registered.

She got up, tapping the teaspoon on her wristbone quite hard. "And in the meantime the Orient Express has been turned into a vehicle asked to pay homage to the most evil men who have ever existed, and things have been so reversed that this beautiful invention now happens to take the lives of young men and women who fight against the extinction of gentleness with an innocence that may never be recovered."

She had to go into another room to walk about, to give herself orders not to indulge herself like this ever again, especially not with Thomas. But every time she heard a shortwave radio going in the basements of the little shops she could obviously think only of the airwaves sending signals from the BBC to wireless sets hidden at risk of death in cellars all over Europe. The muezzins calmly calling to prayer in Turkey could become a sound that was much at odds. Forty percent of the Istanbul minority population was Jewish. The plights of the minorities in Istanbul had none of them been eased by the War. She came back to Thomas and sat down, drew up her knees to her chin and looked at the room, the shutters that splintered the brilliant light of the Bosphorus on the ceiling, the plate glass doors with nineteenth-century engraving on them. Then she pulled his left wrist to her and laid the cool of his watch face against her eyes as she had once laid draughtsmen on his. A piece of paper fluttered out of his pocket as she made the movement.

Her own drawing. A map. The bank, saying "You are here." Arrows to her house, "I am here." A thick blue line for the Bosphorus.

"You should burn this," she said.

"I like having it. Also I keep losing my way every time I come. What are the figures on the back? You gave me the map in a hurry and part of the reason I kept it was because the notes looked valuable, but they don't mean anything to me." She was in the habit of writing figures with circles around them as some people doodle, and said so. "I thought they might be code," he said, easily enough.

"Did the German ambassador respond to your note?"

"He's a mannerly friend to you, isn't he? He asked me if I had time to come to the Embassy for a sherry. He talked mostly of you."

"But what about the German occupation pamphlets?"

"That's where he's such an adroit diplomat. Somebody less skillful would have thought he could best push the affair under the carpet by using an underling. By talking to me himself he told me everything and nothing on the highest authority. I think they call it being civilized."

"Which he is. Didn't he give you any clues at all?"

"He simply took everything in his stride. I'm totally convinced it doesn't matter. That's diplomacy working."

"Did you get the feeling it was a blunder by intent?"

"Nothing to go on."

"Do *you* think it means that Turkey's next on the list?"

"He thanked me for the information, laughed, said it was probably quite vital, and that the other seven pamphlets might well have gone to Wales."

"What language?"

"English, of course."

"He goes from language to language in midsentence if he needs to when he's at a big reception. It's like listening to someone with the gift of tongues."

"He seems to think of you as a sort of goddaughter."

"It's one of his gifts. He makes everyone feel particular."

Thomas waited a while and then said, "You are."

"Enough about diplomacy. Would you like to go to Göreme?"

"No outings until I've done a proper day's work at last. I can't seem to get going. Everybody here seems to have his mind on something else."

"The War. It's not your fault. America will be in the War all too soon and then I'm fearful you'll be called up at once."

"I'm twenty-eight."

"I suppose they may take a while to get to you."

Thomas's mind was on the bank. "I haven't been working. If I were me I'd fire me." He got up.

She kissed him at the door and said, "We *will* go to Göreme."

"We will indeed," he said, walking fast in the direction of the bank, "whatever Göreme is."

He had a good afternoon, and then went to an American film with Turkish subtitles on the way back to her place. He left halfway through, impatient to be with her, and a boy two rows behind him followed him for a quarter of a mile and slipped a note into his pocket before he passed him.

Catherine read it. "It's a ransom note from someone. Wanting the ninety-three books in batches of seven and promising you two thousand dollars for each batch, delivered to the bookshop after hours."

"You're sure you've read it right?"

"Yes."

"Seven doesn't go into ninety-three."

"No."

"So what do I do?"

"It's the bookseller trying you out."

"He might've been prompted by someone wiser."

"Still ignore it. Burn it."

He looked again at the note and put it under the insole of his right shoe. "I'd rather not lose it."

"It'll slip," said Catherine.

"I'll get my secretary to gum it."

"That's top secret work."

"You don't think I'd have anything but a top secret

secretary. She's top secret because she's quite miraculously unobservant. You'd have to ransack the world to find her equal. What is this Göreme?"

She pulled out a photographic book from a pile on a cushion by the window. But he decided to watch her instead of looking at it.

"Did you get any sleep while I was away?" he said.

"I don't need to sleep when I know you're coming back."

"How unhappily are you married?" he said.

"We're better apart at the moment, that's all."

"I'm not good at suspension."

"Everything for the moment has to do with being able to stand suspension."

"That's one of the things you seem to know."

"It's not anything restrictively European."

"No, but Americans do like to get on with it." He anticipated her obviously silent riposte about coming into the War, and said, "Roosevelt has a hard time with Congress."

"I understand why you asked about Jean-Pierre." She played with a flower from the garden that had been put on the tray. "As I promised you before, the fact of you and me isn't taking anything away from him." There was a change in her voice, and she said, "This weekend. Göreme. A plan."

Catherine and Thomas explored Göreme on horseback, riding across the sandy desert until they reached the mass of ancient stone cones with slit windows where the earliest Christians had taken shelter to live out their lives in meditation. Their dwellings, made of the natural but quite unlike anything else in nature that Thomas had seen, sprouted up from the sand in the shapes of half-melted snowmen.

"The moon probably looks like this," said Catherine.

"The moon's as cold as any stone."

"Falstaff?"

"Well, Shakespeare is read in America, you know. I didn't do business management at Harvard."

"I should think you did English literature, didn't you?"

"And history." He said something swift in Old English, a memory repeated not for hearing, and then spoke in his ordinary American voice again. His accent was a little Southern, light and firm. "There wouldn't be early Christian churches and monasteries on the moon. It takes *homo sapiens* to be superstitious."

"The light's cutting into my eyeballs like razor blades," she said. He was already wearing goggles like an early pilot's. He reached into her shirt pocket and said, as he was putting her dark glasses over her eyes, "Had you forgotten I reminded you to bring them? And that's sand in your eyeballs, darling. Not razor blades. You're not imagining that it hurts."

Catherine had a shotgun under her arm. Thomas eyed it. Not a woman to fool around with.

The sandy wind was blowing her shirttails, which were outside her jodhpurs for coolness. She flapped the shirttails with the back of the shotgun and then looked up at a stork that was being tossed in the air like a gull. She raised her shotgun. Not toward the stork. It was Thomas who had a bad flash of a second. Take care that the heat hasn't got to her. Then he called himself a loon, and then she shot at the top of a tree in the opposite direction.

Thomas said, "You're much loved."

Catherine said, "Who by?"

"Me, of course." Startled to be asked. He had a way of speaking a little aside from himself. It occurred to her, not for the first time, that the habit of unlinking himself from what he felt was a matter of shying away from impulses he had schooled himself not to voice.

So she held him for a moment instead. "Mind that shotgun," he said nervously.

"You say it as if I were cooking dangerously, in a long scarf. I've never shot a living thing. Or gone haywire in the kitchen, which seems to be every man's nightmare of women run amok in what's historically a male chef's territory."

She seemed to be defending herself against him, he thought, but she's muddling me with some other man. Has Jean-Pierre shouted at her unkindly?

I'm muddling him with midnight feasts with Jean-Pierre long ago, she thought, and remembered a ridiculous tirade of pomp from Jean-Pierre when she had cooked a soufflé in a muslin dress against yells about the inflammability of muslin that, for a less instinctive cook, would have led to a very unrisen soufflé. She remembered how the soufflé had turned out, and the eating of it together in soft armistice. But even to remember it seemed to be letting down Thomas. They pulled themselves out of their separate thoughts and Thomas raised his face to the wind like a pointer's.

"I never thought I'd feel like this," he said.

"How?"

"Light."

"Darling, do you have to come all the way to a desert full of the bones of early Christians to feel light?"

Thomas said, "On your cushions—"

"—our cushions—"

Thomas said, "—I can't get away from thinking about work. About the oceans between us."

"What oceans, not to be literal?"

For once he was as silent as she usually was. Eventually she said, "Our pasts?"

"Things in the head."

"It's true no one travels without luggage."

"You travel with steamer trunks undeclared."

"It's an illusion. It's in here." She tapped her head. "Cabin luggage. Like anybody else." She tapped his forehead in turn gently. "There's everything in there. The substance of a whole life so far."

THOMAS'S MAIL

Darling Jane,

Thank you for your letter. It got here yesterday. Heaven knows how much we're censored. And also there's something you're not saying. Is it the children? Aren't they getting on with their stepfather? I should tell you that I'm having an affair with a Frenchwoman here. As usual, you'd probably get on. That's the cliché about situations like this, isn't it? You'd also be able to tell me, I guess, what there is going on in her that I can't understand. It can't just be the enigmatic East. She happens to be very beautiful. She's married to a Frenchman who's something diplomatic. (Vichy, of course.) She's a model wife, she's witty and smart, forthright in the way you and I always liked, but there's something hidden about her, though not secretive. Not like anyone I've ever met. She's dramatically silent. She seems to have a lot going on but I can't tell what it is. I figure she's just promiscuous and I'm not very good at coping with that. Maybe Americans really are as puritanical as we're supposed to be. Anyway, I'm not just about to hire a private eye. There are too many of them hanging around Istanbul already. Intriguers, wheeler-dealers, cats. Has the kids' cat had her litter yet? You've been on my mind and I guess one never stops feeling married to someone. Hope you're all okay.

Best, or whatever we say now you're married again,

Thomas.

Dear Thomas,

I didn't show the children your letter because of the contents but they saw the envelope and were pleased you'd been in touch. Yes, the cat (you've probably forgotten the name by now) has had her litter. Adorable creatures, seven of them, we gave away all but two. The children send you their love across the water and everyone hopes that all is well with you. You sound as if you're into things up to your ears! Feel free to write whenever you want. I can't imagine the lady. Sounds very Mata Hari!

In a rush,
Jane.

Dear Jane,

Sorry. I realize from my letter I shouldn't have involved you. Here are a slew of pictures of Turkey for the children. Suppressing an irresistible desire to say "X marks the spot and wish you were here" and other old-time vacation things. As you can imagine—or maybe you can't—this isn't at all a vacation place. Send me a note of what would be good presents for the children (for their Christmas that the War *won't* be over by). And your news. The bank address always finds me.

Ever,
Thomas.

Dear Thomas,

Your letter went off like a firecracker. About Xmas presents for the kids, Chris first said that he'd like Turkey with Greece which may have been his first gruesome joke—I'm not too hot on int. affairs but I assume it is gruesome there, everything is at the moment—and then said could he have either a train with real smoke or Turkish sweetmeats, which he's heard about somewhere. I was surprised because we try not to talk about you too much for the obvious reasons. Bringing up thoughts of a broken home is always psychiatrically bad, Bob and I have agreed. We must protect them. Anyway, hope you have a nice Xmas yourself (with the enigma lady?). Hope that crossword-puzzle psyche is coming out for you. Though actually I'm not sure if they celebrate Christmas in Istanbul. Do they? I can't imagine this place. Is it fun? It's such a long way away and we're such a long time ago.

> Ever,
> Jane.

Dear Jane,

Will study the Christmas present problem, to which things seem to have been reduced between us. I guess that's the sort of failure to understand you that was the trouble all along. My fault, it seems, as usual. I'd wished not to dissemble but I also have no wish to intrude and obviously I did. How odd: It doesn't seem a long time ago to me at all, but I guess that's the way things go.

> Best to you all,
> Thomas.

So, needing a confidante, Thomas could only take counsel of himself. He hardly went to his flat any longer, except as a bachelor's apparently chosen bunkhole to try to track down his laundry. He found himself getting rather solemn about his laundry. Had Byron's great love affairs ever reduced to questions of laundry?

6

◆

ONE day he came to Catherine's unexpectedly early for lunch and found her in the hallway talking to Françoise.

"You do have near images in your maids," Thomas said when they were alone. "I get a shock when I see them wearing your dresses."

"They're not maids, they're Françoise and Agnès. I give them dresses because I'm older and I've accumulated stuff. They came with hardly anything."

"Who's Agnès?"

"She's sixteen. Françoise's younger sister. I did introduce you, I remember. She's a refugee from the South of France, darling. She only just made it."

"She looks at you as if she's got a schoolgirl crush, to put it neutrally."

"But I'm not at all neutral about either of them. They're like family. I teach Agnès Turkish and the piano. She's got to be able to speak Turkish or she'll never make any friends here. Also there's a big gap between the sisters at the moment because of their ages."

"I haven't even seen your piano. I've only seen the harpsichord and the clavichord."

"The piano's in another room. Be soothed." She smiled

61

at him as they went into one of the downstairs rooms and said, "The instruments need different degrees of humidity. As it is they need tuning all the time in this climate."

"I've heard you. Most people need a professional tuner. Is there anything you can't do?"

She turned round and said, "Blimey. Don't be cranky. I do know that perfection's exasperating and don't think I've got it."

"You've everything I long for except the art of including me."

"Sweetheart, there's nothing you can't be part of."

"Except your past."

"Or something." Pause.

"What's the something?" he said.

"You have got an instinct, dove," she said. It was all she could allow herself. She leaned her head against him.

He looked down at the top of her head. "Do you realize you haven't even asked if I've been married before?"

"I knew it hadn't been altogether happy, that's all."

"Goddamn! How did you know anything? And it *was* happy, then. Nearly everything about it. We had a capacity for happiness. In America together then. My ex-wife and I. The fact that it's not the same now doesn't mean that it wasn't wonderful at the time. How *do* you know, anyway?"

"Someone told me. Someone who seemed fond of you."

"Who?"

"A girl at the American Consulate, I think. This place is too full of gossip. And I thought you'd rather not be catechized about it by me."

"Catherine, darling girl, please don't be wise on my behalf."

He left the house saying he hadn't got time for lunch, that he never before had had lunches with anyone except when he was working with them. He didn't see that she was again left leaning her head, on the cool of the banister this time, as if she had a temperature. She laid a tray for their dinner together, tried to leave a message at the bank for him, found there was no reply. He came back at seven, apologetic, and found a note from her sending love, saying she'd had to go to a diplomatic party, had tried to reach him at the bank, would be back at eight.

He wandered about the house and found her dumb keyboard that he remembered seeing on the Orient Express, leaning against the wall like a wooden leg. He played a hesitant scale on it and found it strange, this instrument promising sound but emitting nothing. He had always admired her for clinging to it, for the perseverance it represented in pursuit of a gift she simply happened to have and never put to any use. This brought him back to remembering something that a visiting Frenchman had said years ago in New York, that American education was in danger of regarding every talent as useless if it was not demonstrably furthering a career. "To you," said the man insufferably to his hospitable audience, "everything is grist." Many a Europhobe had been made that day by this spinsterish voice of academe.

The reception Catherine was going to was at the American Consulate. The British ambassador was, as usual, especially cordial to her. He caught her constant polite shakes of the head at proffered miniature frankfurters in dough and took two on her behalf, eating them fast and speaking intermittently. Always with warm heed, always of nothing that would make the newspapers, as only diplomats can. He talked interestingly for at least five minutes around the topic of frankfurters cooked in this fashion. They reminded him, he said at the end, of dim-sum in Peking.

"I didn't know you'd been *en poste* in China," said Catherine.

"Years ago," he said. "Another thing you wouldn't know was that I was at your christening. How is your father?"

"He left just before the fall of Paris. He managed to find a Peugeot and paid all the money he had for it and then of course there wasn't any fuel in the tank. He walked to the Midi, hitchhiking by car when he could. He spent quite a long time with a great painter's son who had a Peugeot that did have some fuel, and he had a stack of Cézannes in the boot. The trunk."

"And where is your father now?"

"In Los Angeles. So is the painter's son."

"I'm surprised about the son's being in Los Angeles by choice. You mean Jean Renoir, don't you?"

Catherine looked at him gratefully, as if she had found some old relation who knew and remembered everything about her and, indeed, a very great deal else, though he never exhibited it. "Well, I was surprised too, but Renoir says he loves Los Angeles. Everything about it except that it's a crime to loiter. In my last letter from my father he said that Renoir had been picked up by the police for walking and he told my father that he thought that this was all wrong, that most of the great ideas in the world had been born of loitering. Including the idea of democracy, which was born of loitering in the agora."

Diverting as necessary for a moment to dim-sum, because the hostess was in hearing, the British ambassador then said, "Please send your father my very best wishes. We walked across Nuristan together when we were at Oxford." Tactful man, he had made no mention of Jean-Pierre and his country's attitude to Vichy. The British ambassador deduced what he wanted from Catherine's presence, prohibited if one were to take protocol strictly, and asked no questions.

"As I was saying, one doesn't speak of what's on one's mind," said Catherine. The British ambassador looked at her for a swift moment, concerned, for she was asserting having said something out loud that she had never uttered. Plainly it was hard for her not to. He could see that she was putting a gag on herself. Her uprightness could never be in question, in this wise old man's opinion, but he wished he might be an ear for her.

A soprano was singing at the end of the room. The ambassador decided to spend a few more moments with Catherine to see her back in command. "The singer's a pupil of Nadia Boulanger," he said. "I remember hearing you playing the harpsichord when you were five. You looked like Nannerl Mozart." He laughed. "I can see you want me to say Wolfgang." He narrowed his eyes, which were very much the eyes of a mountaineer, creased around the sides by looking at bright snows. There could be only one of him.

He thought again, watched her, and saw much going on in her mind. "No. I'm wrong, I think. There may well be more than a little of Wolfgang in you. I hope I shall live long enough to see the world benefiting from it."

He was quite serious. Good man, he never dwelt on a point. After quietly raising her spirits so that she felt he could carry out all manner of solitary tasks even when no end was promised, let alone a result, he spoke swiftly and generously of minorities, apparently talking of minorities in Istanbul but managing to extend it to something he seemed to grasp of her position.

The soprano's voice was not a good one. "You were thinking of your father, weren't you," he said.

"Naturalized now," she said.

"Are you lonely for him?"

Pause.

"A lot of us are lonely at the moment, aren't we?" she said, including diplomats, as he understood, "and any American must feel very much one of a minority group for the time being." He had heard about Thomas, asked nothing. He led her smoothly to speak of the soprano's performance. A bystander, who had been listening all too carefully, said, "Do forgive. I was going to say how pleasant it is to hear French spoken with such cultivation. Or cultivatedness, is it? It's ages since I've been in England. I had English nurserymaids, of course."

The intruder was Hilda, the swift briber glimpsed at Thomas's bank and long since identified by Catherine. Well dressed, strict-faced. She reminded Catherine of the English nanny she had suffered as a small child in Paris. Missing Thomas acutely and longing to be gone, but not wanting to be caught looking at her watch, she said, " 'Good, better, best, never let it rest, till the good is better and the better best.' Did you ever get that one in the neck from an English nanny?"

The British ambassador had moved on. His aide-de-camp quietly kept his eyes on a woman behind Catherine.

"Do join us," he said to Hilda, stranger though she was to him. "These little hot dogs are delicious. Oh, bother," and he suddenly pushed Catherine down to the floor by the shoulder, "that's my lighter and I've got back trouble. Would you rescue it?" The glass in Hilda's hand splintered, hit by a bullet from a gun with a silencer. The aide-de-camp quickly pocketed the bullet. Hilda dabbed with a Kleenex at the wine that had spilled on her dress. "Doesn't matter!" she kept saying. In the crowded hubbub, no one had noticed a thing. Catherine stayed bent to the floor till her teeth stopped chattering. Who wanted her life? A fanatic? An enemy to Jean-Pierre? To her? Even some terrifying bungler?

"Rare thing, that," said the aide-de-camp. "The soprano must have hit high A. These glasses must be crystal. Is that pretty dress washable?"

The unknown woman spoke for the first time. "Poor you," she said. "You must send the bill to the caterers. Serve them right for not using cheaper glasses. I should think it was probably some local Jew with a water pistol, shouldn't you? The Jews here are a dangerously large impurity even though they hate the Turks. The usual chip on their shoulders."

The aide-de-camp said, "The stain's gone. Superb fabric. All's well that ends well." Everyone knowing that things had barely begun. There was no question who the shot had been intended for: Catherine's equal danger now was to show that she knew it, as the aide-de-camp well understood. There also seemed no question that the Kleenex dabber and the anti-Semitic woman were in league.

Catherine said, shaking hands with the A.D.C., "I've got to go. What bad luck about your back," by which he understood exactly what she meant him to: that she was thanking him for saving her life.

"As our American friends say, 'A'byssin'ya,' " he said.

She said, "I think the heat's got to me."

"Or the soprano," said Hilda, making much of the stained-dress plight. "And I've also lost my drink."

"How remiss of me," said the A.D.C. tightly, getting her another one. Fighting his every instinct not to let Catherine walk home on her own, he saw her to the door and said quietly, "We don't know much about her. Gets asked to every diplomatic party going, knows the ropes socially, but odd-jobs as a palmist or something. Whether she's a nut or just blending with the local coloring, that shot was real. For

God's sake watch out. Don't look anxious. People on hard times are dangerous." At that remark only, she flinched.

Catherine walked home quickly, aware that she was being followed by someone in high heels. She chose to loiter once or twice outside the little shops in her neighborhood, quelling her sense of peril, which had been a familiar of her life lately, and thinking instead of the talk that had passed about minorities. Unidentifiable from the back, the woman quickly passed and walked in front of her, carrying a copy of the German High Command phrase book alongside her bag, putting it into the bag as she walked by and turning her face away. Catherine slowed down. Sukru was across the street, holding a wild cat. The woman crossed the road to him and gave him the book without speaking. Then she walked out of sight. Catherine decided to nod only to Sukru and went back to her house.

7

♦

SHE found Thomas asleep.

"Where've you been? I've missed you," he said.

"You were asleep, though." She curled up beside him on her big red cushions.

"But where've you been?"

"I had to go to a reception."

"Without me! You know how I long to get out."

"You'd have been bored. There was a lot of small talk avoiding the War and what people call 'an incident.' Somebody shot somebody under cover of a soprano breaking a glass with a high A."

"Was the shot at you?"

"I shouldn't think so."

Thomas felt afraid for her, but afraid to word his own questions. He thought in tabloid headlines. The Manhattan that work daily whisked him to was a street-talk world full of dangers, but even so it was easier to cope with than the veiled threats surrounding him here. Heaven knows what he was in rivalry with. Some past lover? Europe, perhaps? The War? He felt in the midst of something he would never unravel, when Catherine was forthcoming above all. He longed for something light, blithe, peaceful, and found he was naming the very qualities of Catherine herself.

"*A* midnight raid on the icebox?" said Catherine, quick to read him. Icebox, not fridge, because he was clearly homesick.

"Could we really have something now? Out of hours?" The question told her that he was feeling straitjacketed, a new boy at some school where bullies had found in him their perfect victim. "What would be your favorite thing to have? As long as it's not peanut butter and jam sandwiches."

"That's just what I would like. Why not? Anyway, it's jelly. But why not?"

"Because I haven't got, we haven't got—"

"We? How good."

"We haven't got—"

"We don't have—"

"Any peanut butter or any jam."

It went fast and cheerfully, a musical canon, a cat chasing its tail. Then Catherine said, with due seriousness, "Shall I make us a *salade niçoise?*"

"Is the lettuce safe?"

"What do you mean? That it might have high explosives in it?"

"No. I mean, is it going to give us something?"

Catherine kissed him. "Would you rather have *oeufs mollets?* I'm ravenous."

They went down to the kitchen. Catherine was wearing a red shift. "You're too skinny to be ravenous," said Thomas. "And I love you more than tongue can tell. What are *oeufs mollets?*"

"Cold soft-boiled eggs."

Thomas said, unconsciously stepping backward, "Do the yolks run?"

"Slightly." She saw an extreme case of food alarm and said, "In all compassion I could make them hard-boiled. Though it would be a cheat, you understand."

A boon time for fooling, the middle of the night in a kitchen. And then Catherine took two eggs to boil out of the fridge, dropped one of them, and became totally impassive. Thomas said, after looking into the fridge, "Darling, it's okay, there's another box." She shook her head and went on to boil one egg only.

"I don't get it. It's only an egg gone, which lets me off having to face one. So everything couldn't be better."

She said grittily, "We'll plough our way through half an egg each."

"I'd just as soon not."

"Half each."

Thomas took over. "We really cannot, repeat cannot, have a fight about which of us is not to have half an egg that both of us vehemently don't care a damn about. That's higher mathematics, proving three negatives. What on earth are you thinking about?"

She spun round to him and put her arms round his neck to say, "Sorry sorry sorry. You've rescued it."

"I still don't know what you went into a coma about. Dropping one egg."

"I was thinking of eggs in France. There aren't any. All over occupied Europe there aren't any." She thought about friends in the underground.

Upstairs with the tray, she said, "I once knew a three-year-old who had a terrible temper and was shrieking himself into hysterics about something. He was knocking his head against the wall so hard that his mother thought he was going to concuss himself. I got her out of the room and we listened outside and after a minute the child stopped shrieking in the middle of a sob and said, 'Why doesn't someone come and stop me making this horrible noise?'" She paused, still felt too strongly about the occupation to risk kissing him without crying, and said, "Thank you for stopping me."

Thomas put his arm around her. "It wasn't a noise in this case, it was your silence. You do retreat into the most petrifying silences. I can't find you."

After eating a great deal of *salade niçoise,* Catherine went to sleep. Thomas was alert, waiting for her to waken, knowing her catnaps by now. She suddenly sat up. Thomas put his hand on her.

"What's the matter?" he said.

"Nothing."

"You looked as if you were about to leap up and run."

"I expect I was rethinking *salade niçoise.*"

Or a whole string of things it's connected with, he thought. "Do you make it for Jean-Pierre?"

"*No.* He has Scotch and a chicken sandwich at midnight and then porridge or kedgeree at seven forty-five in the morning. Anything between would disturb his sleep."

"How does he sleep?"

"Heavily. Anchored with coded cables and memos." Pause.

"It must be difficult to be married to someone who sleeps all the way through the night. Why don't you ever tell me about Jean-Pierre?"

"Have you got a comb somewhere?" She turned her tousled head round to him.

"Stay just like that." He ran his fingers through her hair as he had done on the terrace many moons ago, holding her a little away from himself as though he were looking at a photograph of her.

"What do you owe Jean-Pierre?" he said.

"Our past," she said after a pause. There was another pause, longer, and then she said, "Why do you need to know?"

"Because he has a lot to do with you."

"He has no liability, none whatever, for the way I live and act now. I think that's true." A way of inspecting her words that she had.

"Then who has?"

"Could we not talk?"

He pulled her down to the cushions, where she sat like a little girl with her chin on her knees. She smiled at him and nodded. All the same, she got up after a moment and went out to the kitchen. To the sound of saucepans being washed, his malaise came back.

Next day Thomas went to the bank early, worked with effort through the long lunch hour when no tellers, no secretaries, no clients were there, tried to keep himself awake with some cold Turkish coffee, went abruptly to sleep on a desk of papers that turned to feathers in a dream. So much for his homeland's turning away of coffee after dinner "Because I won't sleep." Coffee, the instant sedative. He woke even more tired, tried to introduce briskness in himself as though he were at home by watering down Turkish coffee to the strength of his usual American breakfast cups, wanted to sleep more than ever. The Turkish lunch contagion. He got up with pretended resolution and left the office carrying his attaché case. As he walked to Catherine's house he found himself being followed. There was no thought in his mind that the follower was a pickpocket, a paid scent hound for one side or the other, some beneficiary of war's market in loyalties. Best, in this blazing daylight—well, most natural, most unsuspectingly neutral, most representative of his country's present position in a "European" war—best to turn round and face the tracker. The peril turned out to be Sukru, now doubling as his bank's mail delivery boy. "As your personal mailboy I shall describe my full new responsibilities," Sukru had explained gallantly to Catherine in a Turkish that seemed to be a translation from a new and highly endeavored English. "Forever the friend of you, madame, and always the right hand of your garden, I am now also representing Mr. Thomas Drake as his private courier."

Sukru carried a packet of mail for him and pointed up to a sign just above them saying "Fortune-teller" in four languages. As the boy wouldn't release the packet until Thomas made signs of obeying the finger ordering him to go upstairs, and as the packet had airmail envelopes in it from America that he pined for, Thomas went to the stairs, and was then allowed to take the packet. The boy oversaw his progress upward.

There was no electric light. As befits wheelers-and-dealers in superstition, thought Thomas, feeling not at all under a curse. The top step had a more shallow rise than the others. He fell forward a little and found he was already in someone's room. Blinds drawn. Thick velour curtains. A low-hung red glass lamp over a cluttered table that was covered with a musky wool tapestry rug, and a woman sitting at it looking at a photograph apparently without taking note of his entrance.

"What's your name?" he said.

She was swathed in scarves half covering her long face, which was not severe as it had seemed before to Catherine but now strikingly sad. "Ah," she said, eyes staying on the photograph. A small girl of about three, wearing a fresh white muslin dress that lifted his spirits in the dank room, was wandering about eating grapes that she had dangled behind her ears in obvious imitation of Hilda's long green glass earrings.

Hilda said, "Yes?"

Thomas said, "The little boy signaled me up here. You wanted me."

"On the contrary, you have been needing to see me for some time. My charge is ten dollars, as you are an American."

Thomas handed her a ten-dollar bill with contempt and held to silence about her arcane pretensions. As he had never registered the woman in the bank, her behavior as though she knew him was unpleasant, like her assumption that she knew his mind without asking questions.

"You have been wondering about this woman," she said. She turned the photograph to him. It was one of Catherine with an older man, sitting on a stone wall together, with famous Italian buildings behind them. Catherine was laughing, holding the man's hand, looking up at him.

"You want to know about this man, don't you." Pause.

"I've never seen him."

"Of course not. He is your mistress's husband."

The child, who had been clinging on to an open drawer for support, suddenly fell and cried. Hilda watched without helping. She seemed quite untethered to anything normal. Thomas, shaking, picked up the child and put her on his lap. Hilda was implanting something wild in the room. Thomas thought of many things at once, as one does. His children, the refugees in the Bosphorus ships, the look on Catherine's face in the photograph. Less vital, because he despised this woman for playing, the question of how she seemed to know him without even bothering to look at him, let alone how she knew that he loved Catherine.

"What's this about a mistress?" he said.

She moved her hands among the fringes of the red lampshade. The hands were white and veined, freighted with gold and amber rings. They had the look of the hands of millionaire women at casinos at dawn, ageless old women who had gambled every night since the beginning of time and seemed never to have seen daylight. "All Istanbul knows your connection," she said. "You have no need to deny your need of me."

He felt himself crumbling. Perhaps asking her questions didn't matter, he thought, even though a strong part of his mind told him that he was crumbling further in thinking such a thing. "Is he a violent man?" he said, in spite of his doubt. Perhaps a breezy line to her would clear the haze she spread, so he added, "I might as well put my cards on the table." His eyes drifted to her tarot cards and fixed on one of them: an androgynous figure, apparently boneless, like a Pre-Raphaelite drawing, clasped in immobility by scarves that swathed the figment from chest to thighs. Everything strange. A male Ophelia dragged from the river bandaged in trailing weeds, strangled by soft winds that fluttered the weeds but held no oxygen. He coughed and gasped, and then found the breath in this stagnant air to say with strength again, "I asked, is he a violent man?"

Hilda turned the photograph back to study it again herself. Pretense, folly. "An interesting question. I should say, yes, a bloodless man, with not much passion in him but much trouble."

Thomas clenched his muscles against surprise attack, even though he knew he was only feeling embattled in obedience to this woman. "You have here an audacious nose," she said, "severe hair, the eyes of a wolfhound with the mouth of a trout."

The child said, "What is trout?"

Hilda kept silent and looked only at Thomas, who chose to take a long time to say anything. At last he said to the child, "A small delicate fish."

Hilda said, "Your close involvement is clear. You were right to seek me. This man is one she's taken pleasure in. Pleasure she may never have known from you. That's what's on your mind. Tell me what you think it is that he gives her."

"Beautiful clothes. A beautiful house."

"But not her beauty."

"Which is astonishing," he said. She was pressing speed on him.

"But why does she bewilder you?" she said.

"Because I don't know where her stamina comes from."

"Stamina," said Hilda, coercing him without his noticing it any longer. "And to add to that, the house is hers, the money for the clothes is hers, the taste for the clothes is hers, the talent for musical composition is hers. Why do you think that is?"

"How do you know? And how did you know that she was musical?" said Thomas.

Hilda ignored the question and went on, "Everything is hers. You are hers. We must ask ourselves why."

"I'm my own man."

"You're drawn by her strength. Your work is going downhill. You're frightened of slippery slopes. You're frightened of her strength."

"You're a hypnotist," he said, "presenting yourself for gain as a professional fortune-teller under false pretenses." He lost his grip, didn't hear that he was being absurd. He said, driven, "In my country that would be a case for the law."

"But you're entirely cut off from your country. Your statement about her strength remains. The strength does not come from you." Even then, narrowly stopping himself from accusing her of brainwashing, he registered that the statement she called his was hers. He tried turning the tables.

"So you are saying that her strength comes from others," he said. "People I don't know."

"So now you must ask yourself what others," she said. "Your mouth is dry."

"May I have a glass of water?"

The child on his lap gave him a grape, dismantling one of her pretend earrings with generosity. Her blitheness made him say to Hilda, "Istanbul is supposed to be the city of pleasure. Why am I in pain?"

Hilda looked at him without expression.

"Tell me. I'm paying you. You seem to know all the people in her life."

"Perhaps the strength is from people in other countries. Does she talk of Vichy? Of Pétain? Of the Führer?"

"Sometimes."

"She mentions names?"

"Her husband's valet."

"He is Turkish. That is not the answer to our question."

"She doesn't care for him anyway. He is the only person I have ever heard her talk about with disgust. She calls him the toad."

"Go on." He did, bidding himself not to notice that the cant of her trade covered an inquisitiveness about matters outside her compass. She promised anonymity, and balm for an ache, that was all. So he simply went on answering her about the valet and paid no attention to her drift. "If he had the energy, she said once, he would be a Nazi," he said.

"There is our link. Your jealousy should seek the identity of a rival among the Allies." She paused. "It could be here, or it could be someone she is in touch with. My cards don't tell me. You will have to help me. If I am to help you, that is. She knows France well?"

Thomas felt more than ever uneasy, most of all because of his alarm that she might have something to tell him that no one else could. So for all his scorn, he supplied facts. "She's half-French. She went to university at the Sorbonne and before that she was at school in the South of France. Near her grandmother."

Hilda spread out her tarot cards, looked at them, collected them, and asked him to choose one. Hoping to restore himself by cleaving to his real amusement about superstition, he obeyed and drew out a drawing of an elephant raising its trunk to its head, with a crown lying in forest grass. Again the faked Pre-Raphaelite style. Hilda held both hands to her temples melodramatically when he gave her back the card.

"I see a foreign country in the grasses," she said.

"That's an elephant. African or Indian. Naturally it's foreign."

"No. The grasses signify a temperate zone to me. They are in a wind. It is the north wind of distress." He was feeling so at odds with himself that he could only just make himself see the nonsense she was spilling to him. Nor did the recognition of it detract from its witchery. She went on relentlessly, and the single light bulb seemed to get dimmer. "The elephant is a vehicle. I see emphasis in the trunk. Trunk line. That tells us we are looking at an international train, a trunk line train. So. Madame de Rochefauld has dethroned friends, friends robbed of their country or their heritage, banished friends?"

"You mean she has a lover in the French underground? Something to do with the Orient Express?"

He had given her information without knowing it. She had given him something to worry about. False or true, he had no idea.

"It may be a gang," she went on. "A whole group enmeshing her."

She watched him closely and saw him acquiescing so as

79

not to lose his dignity. She was left with the speculation that
Catherine was involved somewhere with an anti-Nazi group,
perhaps in France, though this man might be clever and
might be flaunting a false clue. He was left with the thought
that Catherine might be inconstant by having a lover of old
now left behind in France, permitted by her husband by the
arcane rules governing Parisian society: someone in a hostile
political position who endangered her life because of her
feelings about longevity of private ties.

"We can only be sure," said Hilda, making the old
collusion between torturer and victim, "if you will go
through her Paisley-covered notebook. You have seen this, of
course. You can copy out what you find in it."

"I don't go through private papers. I'm a banker."

"But your personal honor is at stake. You must save her
from herself. She is alone. With your help I see great
happiness ahead for her."

"Could we turn the fans off? I can't think in this noise."

"The noise is faint. Constant, reposeful. The noise is in
your head. You will be quiet when you return with the
reports you will have copied." Hilda made no gesture to turn
off the fans, no gesture even that the session was finished. He
got up and said, "I doubt if we'll meet again. But I'd better
have your name and address."

"I do not care for correspondence. I'm always here."

As Thomas went down into the sunlight he vowed never
to come up these dingy stairs again. Woman of treacherous
judgments, idle slaughters. Who said that? Perhaps some
touched-off memory, perhaps himself putting her to one side.
He disbelieved every word she had said, now that he was out
in the light, and neglected to inspect what he had told her and
the value she put on it.

8

♦

$\mathbb{T}$HOMAS came back to Catherine's house and found her playing Scarlatti on the harpsichord. Françoise was standing at the door listening, a pile of freshly ironed linen over her arms which she handled in a way that made him think for a flash of some Victorian woman holding a baby in long lace christening robes. He brushed past her and she held a finger to her lips. She belonged to the house more than he did. In assertion, he sat down in an armchair covered with a dust sheet. Françoise smiled at him, tiptoed over, and gestured to him to get up so that she could slide the dust sheet away for his comfort. Again she gestured to him, this time to look at the tapestry work on the chair she kept covered against the sun.

Catherine stopped playing and said, "It's my favorite chair in the house. It's even comfortable, or fairly."

"What's the design?"

"Daniel in the lion's den. Yet it was done by Muslims. That's authenticated. It bewilders experts. Muslims stitching a biblical story. And Muslims don't illustrate the human face, either. It's held to be heretical."

Daniel, rather badly sketched for the tapestry workers to fill in, with out-of-proportion biceps and foreshortened legs, was raising his hands upward in a cave full of lions and lion skulls. The lions looked to Thomas like an Old Testament collection of Istanbul's own wild cats. One of them was pretending not to be asleep, resting on his paws a heavy head that had one eyelid a little opened. Another was standing guard, assuming overtime sentry duty in the heat with a scowl on his face that seemed to come not from fury but from balancing the weight of a heavy invisible helmet on a head required to express nullity, as a palatial guard is required to do outside a monarch's entry gate.

"Who's the man at the top of the cave opening?" said Thomas.

"It would be King Darius, wouldn't it?" said Catherine.

"He's got an Egyptian profile. The forehead running straight into the nose. But he's wearing a fez."

"The design isn't that easy to explain. It's a Semitic profile. We're in a tangled part of Europe. This is pretty old, remember."

"Eighteenth century?" said Thomas.

Catherine looked at him to see if he meant it and then said gently, "The experts guess fourteenth century at the latest."

He walked over to the harpsichord and turned Catherine to the sun so that he could say out of Françoise's hearing, "Can't you get rid of that woman hanging about?" Catherine went to Françoise and spoke a few words in French about menus for tomorrow.

"She's Françoise, not 'that woman,'" she said to Thomas afterward. "What's up, darling?"

"She's been through a lot, she's kind, she's silent as mud but she's everywhere. And hell, she was wearing your clothes again."

"Why not?"

"She mimes everything you do."

"She's been with us a long time."

"You said this was *your* house."

"It is. But she's been with us both when I was still going to Ankara. She used to work partly at the Embassy. When France was still hanging out. She speaks Arabic, which helped everyone."

"Hell. All these foreign languages. I should have worked harder at them."

She sat down at the harpsichord again and played some scales. "All right, she's silent as mud, in your phrase. Is it slang?"

"I think I made it up."

"My love, I've never asked where you come from. You're not a New Yorker, I do know that."

"The Virginia tidewater country. You wouldn't know it."

"It seems blindingly obvious that you've got a gift for languages."

"I always wish I'd gone on and done a couple of years of international law."

"It's not too late."

"The War will make it too late."

She thought for a while and then said, "The War makes everything hypothetical. Every thought has to have 'if we survive' built into it."

"You're not a defeatist. That's a defeatist thing to say."

She was playing something now that she seemed to have made up.

"What's that?" he said.

"I've set two catchphrases and I'm trying to get them to go in counterpoint."

"Bach and Handel, or something?"

"No. A tune for two slogans in wartime England.

'Coughs and sneezes spread diseases' and 'Walls have ears.' I can't get it right yet."

"In America with Lease-Lend the 'Walls have ears' one is 'Loose lips sink ships.' "

She tried two quite different tunes against each other, and turned her smile to him. "You've done it. Listen. You sing the bass." She played it twice for him. " 'Loose lips sink ships.' Yes. Now do it a fifth higher." She gave him the note. "Then back to the tonic." He sang it through twice, and then she added her "Walls have ears" phrase in counterpoint.

He went to get them a cool drink and came back to find her writing music fast. "I want to give this to Sukru. Isn't he usually here by now with your stuff?"

The fortune-teller episode, quite forgotten for this respite, filled his mind again. Furtive though it made him feel, he kept quiet about it. "Is that boy really reliable?" was all he allowed himself.

Catherine spread her hands. "Buyable," she said. "He's in confusion. His commitment's to survive." A refugee ship hooted outside, crowded to the rails with people who carried their belongings in brown paper bags, in kerchief bundles. "Like theirs," she said, trying not to spread sadness.

"And yours," he said, on an unmarked question point.

"Ours is, in both cases, more complex."

"In what way? Yours, for instance?"

She merely smiled, gestured calm, addressed an envelope, and put the music inside it. There were stamps at the back of her Paisley notebook lying at the bass end of the piano keyboard.

"Who's it to? A piece of music by airmail with no letter?"

"It doesn't need one. It's for a musicologist friend of mine at the Royal Academy of Music. We write to each other all the time. Music gets through the censors without trouble as long as it's obviously going to someone at a music college."

"How does his get to you?"

"He just writes out the music degree I've got in full. Anyway, everyone here knows that I play things. The letters were opened at first but it must be the same censor all the time because they've been getting through unopened long since. We number the letters between us. Obviously a special cipher clerk was allotted to them but it's a very rank old bit of red herring by now."

"If I were a cipher clerk that's just the time I'd start being careful," Thomas said.

"That's because you're intelligent. Cipher people are jumpy but stupid, on the whole. I do know the one about never underestimating the intelligence of your enemies, but that's true about everyone, not just enemies. The pure enemy is very hard to find. That's what makes Istanbul particularly perilous. Don't let's think that, just because America's bound to find a way of coming into the War sooner or later, you haven't been watched all along." She knew a great deal, thought Thomas, and didn't know at all how much it was. Perhaps she knew everything known and thought it of no account weighed against the incomprehensible. A genius without guy ropes, Catherine. A racing mind with no rival to clock itself against. He fell in love with her all over again and hummed something from his past that she harmonized as he went on the harpsichord, following without ever seeming to be behind.

Next morning, early at the office, he had an appointment with a Swiss client, Monsieur Dindeau. He was a small man with busy legs and the most symmetrical face that Thomas had ever seen. When he sat down, drawing his chair round to a place parallel to Thomas's instead of facing him across the desk, he did it correctively, as though he were an officious hostess rearranging silver considered wrongly placed by a poorly trained parlormaid. On any other day Thomas would have thought himself about to be sacked.

"My firm wishes me to tell you," said Monsieur Dindeau, playing with the combination lock on his briefcase, "that much to our regret your performance in the field of currency conversion has been far from what we should have hoped. Indeed, should have been hoping ever since the onset of hostile activity." Monsieur Dindeau, thought Thomas, invents tenses beyond the dreams of linguistic philosophy, and with all that armory has the gall to name the War by a euphemism.

"I find myself in the midst of regretting that we shall have been come to this. At the same time I find myself, with this mixture of feelings, understanding with fraternal mind that you are preoccupied with occupied Europe. Excuse the repetition, I shall try to rephrase it." This vamp-till-ready pettifogger is playing the prelude to a great aria about giving me the sack, thought Thomas, plunging in.

Coughing in an executive fashion to go with the mood appointed by his opponent, Thomas collected the papers on his desk into three neat stacks and said with a smile, "Of course, it is not for your financial adviser to correct a great bank in the person of yourself, but the calculations you have been sending me are steadily based on a howler."

"Howler."

"Yes. You deal in commodities, but you've entirely neglected the black market options in sugar beet."

"Sugar beet."

"That's the way I've made you a fortune."

"I don't seem to have that note." Monsieur Dindeau

operated his combination lock, fussed through his papers, failed to find what he was looking for, and said, weakening fast, "Before we should have terminated our cooperation—in short, our employment of you—I shall have needed to see through all your papers, including this missing one you speak of."

Thomas knocked lightly on his forehead with his index finger. "Luckily that one's in writing and we have a copy, but many of them are in here in my head. A great deal of the work I do for you would be too expensive for you if I were to put it on paper."

"Paper."

"So I choose to remember. It is a more efficient way. And also more portable."

"A head being more portable than a desk and a secretary." Monsieur Dindeau nodded with great comprehension.

Thomas nodded gravely, or as gravely as he could in the circumstances of this talk, rose, shook Monsieur Dindeau's hand, and said, "Your affairs are prospering. You'll find the misapprehension you're under fully banished when you read the memo sent you on the tenth of the month last year. My best wishes. Please feel free to write if I can be of any other assistance." He called his secretary and asked her to give Monsieur Dindeau the copy of the crucial memo while Monsieur was waiting in her outer office. "And some coffee? I hope it isn't too strong for your taste. We live on it here. When in Rome—"

"Yes indeed."

Aghast at his own performance, though he had told the man the droll commercial truth in his triumphant sugar beet sentence, Thomas made his apologies and hurried out of the bank with the Christmas presents for his children in his Manhattan imported-leather briefcase.

He went to the American Consulate, where he had made

an arrangement to see the consul, a blond young woman called Mary-Ann whose brother he played squash with at the Racquet Club in New York.

Home territory, he expected to feel, but things had shifted, and he found for the first time that he was just as much at home in the cobbled streets of Istanbul. After due protocol and no agitation, he found Mary-Ann behind a laden desk. "Hi there," she said. "You're dead on time. No one's ever on time in Istanbul."

"I've got through something faster than I expected. Now, look, you must tell me honestly. One of the two parcels is fairly unwieldly. Can the diplomatic pouch really be used to send the things?"

"No problem."

He drew out the wrapped presents, labeled.

"Fragile?" she said.

"One's a toy train. A wheel came off at once but I think I've fixed it. Istanbul in the War isn't the place to look for a toy train."

"Nor anytime. Where did you buy it?"

"I found a cobbler who made it. It's interestingly slightly wrong. More like a ferryboat crossed with a farm cart. But the painting is wonderful. I think he said they were vegetable dyes in the paints."

He took her out to lunch. They spoke of the War, of Lease-Lend. He asked her about Pétain and de Gaulle, the Maquis. She spoke no more French than he did. The ever-present possibilities of disguises, spying, double-dealings, faded for the moment.

9

◆

AT ease, and in command of things once more, Thomas lay on his back on the cushions in the upper room at Catherine's. Sukru yelled from the Bosphorus outside. Catherine went out onto the terrace and let down a basket for the ad hoc mail delivery.

"Many private letters for Mr. Thomas from America," said Sukru gaily in proud semblance of English. "Of course, I couldn't help official people looking at them. But I allowed them no opening of anything. That I did myself. Have you anything for me, Madame de Rochefauld?"

She said something too low for Thomas to hear and came inside with the post, which was nearly all for him. Her own she put beside the bed. "What were you saying to the little Dickensian cadger?" he said as he slit open his mail.

"He's all right as long as you realize he's forced to be buyable. In the circumstances, no family, no school, no one he's allowed himself to trust—"

Catherine was urgently due at Ann Wisner's but it was not her way to show pressure. Agnès knocked at the open door and came in with an ironed petticoat of Catherine's.

"De Gaulle's in London," said Catherine. Agnès smiled and raised her head. Pause. Nothing needed to be said between them.

"You remembered my night off, madame?" she said after a moment.

"Sleep late tomorrow."

The young maid smiled, put away the petticoat, and went out.

"What's the trouble?" said Catherine to Thomas.

"Nothing."

"I can't help knowing the people who work here, darling."

"I don't speak French."

Catherine sat in the deck chair near the window, putting aside her lateness at Ann's and thinking that there probably were moments when she unwittingly isolated him from things without meaning to. She held his mail for him, with his sister's airmail letter and envelope on top of the pile.

"I'm sorry," she said. "Remember she's in exile."

"It's okay. All's well. Remember I *chose* to be here," he said. "I just feel inept sometimes at looking after you."

She smiled fast at him and nodded and changed into the red shift with a huge slice of amber on a chain round her neck. "Where are you off to?" said Thomas.

"I'll be back in an hour. I'm going to Ann Wisner's. You remember her. She was on the Orient Express with me. Except that it was long ago." Pause. "A lifetime, or several seasons, whichever shall be the shorter. As some legal agreement might have it. But as we're beyond the law all clauses are cancelable."

"And you are considered by me, or any insurance loss adjusters—ho-hum—however mouse-hearted, not—well, not an act of God, because that to them spells damage, but certainly a benediction, which they wouldn't know about."

* * *

Catherine went to Ann Wisner's carrying her dumb keyboard. Ann's house was, like hers, on the Bosphorus, but it stood on a high cliff above the water. They kissed each other. Now seeing each other much more often since the train journey from Paris, they had come to know each other well enough for Ann to finish with mannerisms of flightiness. She no longer pretended to Catherine that Kemal did the thinking for them both, held the keys of political opinions for them both.

Ann went out into the garden with a pair of gardening shears. Rambler roses were spilling over the roofless garden shed. She started to prune them, and under cover of the pruning adjusted the radio-transmitting antennae that were hidden under the scramble of rose roots, watching Catherine in the room inside for signs about the reception she was getting. Catherine crouched over the radio-transmitting equipment, generally disguised by a big drop-leaf table covered with a pretty Belgian tablecloth and piles of art books.

"How's that?" Ann mouthed.

Catherine nodded. Ann came in.

"You've brought your dumb keyboard this time," she said.

Catherine said, "Could we have coffee while I practice something? I was thinking it out as I came here."

"As long as you promise to play me what you're hearing in your head."

"As soon as it's finished. I want to keep on with what I did yesterday and then radio it through."

As Ann went into the kitchen to make coffee, Catherine played through some words on a dictaphone machine and set them to music on the dumb keyboard. It seemed to go all right. She wrote out the melody and the harmony on two sets of music paper. As they were having coffee, Ann fiddled with the knobs of the radio, which was labeled as being Catherine's property and engraved with Catherine's name and address in case of burglars. "Because it's on my insurance policy," Catherine had said, though of course—as Ann knew—it was to protect Ann from the consequences of owning an illicit shortwave wireless if the Germans were to take over Turkey.

She found her contact in London. Their call signal was "Allo allo allo." It made Ann and her both think of vaudeville, music hall, joyful double acts in stand-up comedy. Catherine fed the message over the air, first by singing the melody and the harmony, then by doing it verbally. "Treble clef, key signature E major, six-eight time, A above middle C crochet, F natural F sharp G natural triplet in quavers, E above middle C minim . . ." and so on for half an hour, receiving replies that finally moved three bars into another key signature.

"It sounds as meaningless to me as a list of stock exchange figures," said Ann at the end of it, snapping off the switches.

"Listen to what your favorite Astaire song sounds like said in words." Catherine did "No Strings, No Connections" in this laborious way. Ann said cheerfully, "Yes, you certainly manage to wreck it. Now salvage it and sing it for me, though I'm not sure it's not irretrievably a man's song." Catherine made a face at that, which Ann agreed with, and sang. Ann listened and nodded happily. "Why don't you just send things by singing them and leave it at that?"

"It's a double check. There's such a lot of distortion. It may be coming out the other end at any pitch."

Ann looked at the dumb keyboard. "There's a piece of paper sticking out."

"I know. It's the end of the paper that will have taken a copy of the notes I struck. I send that off as a triple check."

"Darling, if it were opened it would look very like code."

"And if it were decoded, which wouldn't take much brain because I obviously put in the key signatures and clefs, it would look very like music. I don't think cipher clerks would take much pride in cracking that one." Catherine stayed quietly with Ann for a while. A light on the radio suddenly came to life and Ann flicked on some switches. "Allo allo allo." Catherine sat down among the equipment and took down some music on the music paper she always had in her bag, listening to it with amplifying headphones. The transmission line became too faint to hear before the notes had been double-checked in words. She looked at what she had taken down, and said to Ann, "There's a suggested change because of the singer's range. I'll have to go and play it and probably think of something else." She whistled it and shook her head. "We'll give them a better idea tomorrow." She kissed Ann good-bye, asked if she could leave her dumb keyboard behind this time as she needed to run. On her way back to her house she made a quick detour to a little shoemaking shop. "Traveler's checks cashed. Handmade shoes in Turkish leather," read the sign over the bead curtains. Inside, a man was sitting cross-legged stitching a boot. Catherine said, in Turkish, "Five million Turkish sugar items at the black market rate in exchange for ten million Swiss paper items at the Berlin rate through Algerian heavy." The man said, "Commodity futures, yes," in Turkish; thought; did calculations in his head; and repeated the specifications with a few changes that she wrote down in some shorthand of music notes and letters of the alphabet on a piece of his thin shop stationery. She memorized them, juggled as they now were into a reorder she would recall, and out in the little cobbled street shoved the note into a paper bag of Turkish sweetmeats that she had in her wicker basket.

10

◆

WHEN she got back to her house, there was a message on a little Louis Quinze table just inside the half-open doors. Thomas's handwriting. It said: "I'm going to be working late. Will sleep at the bank's place tonight. Sorry I've been fretful. I really do need longer working hours for both our sakes. Love T. (P.S. *vitello tonnato* tomorrow night? Seen marked in your recipe book.)" And beside it, there was another note in Jean-Pierre's handwriting: "I shall be upstairs waiting for you. J.-P."

He stood at the head of the stairs, having heard her footsteps.

"Catherine." He made no movement toward her, but left her to run up the stairs to him. He held her away. "Who's T.?" he said.

"Are you sure you want to ask?"

"Not if you feel it isn't my business." He lit a Turkish cigarette with a gold lighter she had given him.

"I believe we'll always be one another's business," she said. She knew that he wouldn't reply, but she would always give him the space to.

He made a movement with his right hand toward her, closed it as if accepting something actual, and then opened it palm downward and seemed to be steadying some invisible

95

shivering light object underwater that needed to be tethered to stop it floating up and away out of grasp. Then he led the way into the big upper room and they sat down by the window. Agnès brought in a tray of Turkish coffee and French bread with some cheeses.

"Is this what we want?" said Catherine.

"I asked Agnès for it," said Jean-Pierre. "We haven't met."

"Agnès, this is Monsieur de Rochefauld," said Catherine with difficulty.

"Françoise told me." Agnès held her uniform skirt and made a little bob of a curtsy, unsure of how to behave. "Monsieur has everything he needs, madame?"

"Agnès couldn't join Françoise till the end of 1940," said Catherine. "She had to wait in the South of France for a boat."

"There were thousands hoping to escape," said Jean-Pierre. "Your de Gaulle didn't take great care of them."

"He had a good deal on his mind."

"Agnès, have we still any French brandy in the cellar?" said Jean-Pierre.

Agnès looked at Catherine for confirmation. Catherine smiled and said, "I think there's even some Marc left." While Agnès was finding it, she fetched the draughts board and they began to play in the dying sunlight. The warm evening breeze stirred the muslin curtains. Jean-Pierre tried to make himself at ease on the cushions, but his long legs kept crumbling into awkward angles like a newborn foal's.

"Do you hate lying about on cushions? Men never know what to do with their legs," said Catherine.

"Hence the invention of the chair," said Jean-Pierre. "I'm hardly first generation in having difficulty. It simply isn't very comfortable. This position forces the entire right angle onto the hip joints. The knees are omitted, in spite of being also right-angled joints."

"Yes," said Catherine solemnly, sitting with her knees drawn up to her chin with the greatest of ease and trying to imagine what Jean-Pierre was feeling like. "Is it the sensation of a collapsible ruler that hasn't been folded up properly?"

"To know that, one would have to be a collapsible ruler," said Jean-Pierre, looking at her to see if she were laughing. It had been a long time. They both were. It was all right.

"A collection of male collapsible rulers grumbling about where to put their legs at a picnic is now a vivid possibility," said Catherine.

"If one thinks of Impressionist paintings of picnics, men are never required to eat sitting directly on grass. There is provision of chairs," said Jean-Pierre.

The Marc was brought up. They both had a glass. Jean-Pierre brought his knees up toward his chin as though he had thought of the movement himself. The draughts board was between them. They played with peculiar fierceness, talking between moves. The hollow click of the pieces on the board, the occasional hooting of ships outside, were the only sounds as they played and sporadically talked.

"And who is T.? I've decided I would like to know." He paused with a sweet flash of courtesy between them. "If I may."

"A man in international finance. He's American."

"Where is he?"

"Finishing work and then, according to the note, going to the villa the bank provided him with."

"I'd expected him to be with you this evening."

I have indeed wounded him, even though he pretended I

wouldn't. "It'll be the first time he hasn't been here since we met properly."

"Which is how long?"

"Two and a half years, nearly."

"What's the matter?" Jean-Pierre's voice was peculiarly tender.

"I'm sad for all three of us. I suppose I'm even sad you're not angry about him."

"I'm trying to be glad you've had someone to replace me. We couldn't be together in Ankara at the moment. Feeling about Pétain as you do."

She got up suddenly, looked for her wicker basket, and retrieved the piece of paper with the notes she had made at Ann's house. They belonged in her Paisley notebook beside the bed. The notes she had made at the cobbler's shop she had memorized and put back into her basket to be burned later. As she came back to the draughts game she said, "Anyway, I'd be an embarrassment to you in Ankara."

"What was that in your basket?"

"Some notes." Another pause. "I won't go any further. Nothing secret from you; just something that it will be easier from your point of view not to know about."

They understood where to call a halt to confidences. She said then, with the same readiness to drop her question, "I know that Turkey's going through all the diplomatic motions with Vichy, but where do you stand, darling?" The "darling" was natural between them and neither of them registered it particularly.

"It can't be easy," she went on. His mouth had tightened. "I'd expected you might even resign. You're no fascist pushover."

He said, "I don't see it that way."

So he would go on acting for Vichy, perhaps in some danger, because the regime was gaining in many Turks' dislike. His loyalty to Pétain was unquestionable: he would never waver in that.

"You wouldn't yield in your opinion about de Gaulle, would you?" he said.

She held a silence.

"No, of course you wouldn't." Pause. "Do you miss me?"

Again she stayed silent, though she looked at him with such clarity that he could have picked her up and swept her away for the assurance of concord that her expression gave him. "Darling, you always did use your silences as armaments." She made a move on the board and captured two of his men. He paid not much heed to that, and instead carried on the thinking aloud that he had embarked on. "I hoard them," he said, loving her. "They're valuable to me. They will increase in value."

Catherine turned swiftly from restraint to contempt. "Then you could sell them. Belittling other people's choices to shut up when it's what you have always claimed for yourself as your right."

"At least I'm loyal to my country."

"You think our country is naturally defeatist? You think Pétain is the voice of France?"

"Pétain is the glory of France."

"Giving in to Hitler without a murmur. The Germans simply walked into Paris. Pétain went limp. He needs a gram of madness in him."

"Clemenceau said that."

"I know."

Jean-Pierre leaned back with his hands folded behind his head. "You know too much and say too little."

"Your paradoxes stink." She took that back with a wave of her hand across her mouth.

"So what should we have done instead of Vichy?"

"You don't really want to know. You're just testing me. One-two-three-four testing."

Jean-Pierre looked at the board. "You're winning by miles."

"You didn't notice?"

Catherine went on playing, and poured him some more Marc.

Jean-Pierre said, "No diplomat can have a wife who"— he went on playing, though she had nearly wiped out his men—"disagrees with him about something so fundamental."

Catherine wept, unexpectedly. *"France fell.* It fell because not enough Frenchmen stood firm. Englishmen did. I can't accept that France doesn't fight. If Thomas were a Frenchman, he'd fight."

"Oh, is that his name? Not that it's my business."

Catherine was still crying. "Yes. Thomas. Some people he doesn't like call him Tommy."

"You're being emotional. I don't know you like this."

Catherine amassed more and more captured draughtsmen on her side of the board.

"And the draughtsmen go click, and you pile them up, and you try to make me have a tantrum with your unspoken opinions. You have no right. You have no right to bear other opinions. You have no *right.*"

"Well, I do think differently, and I'm sorry."

"About de Gaulle, or about Thomas?"

Catherine spread her hands, first the right, then the left, and shook her head at the impossibility of explaining anything to this man of rage and reason whom she unfailingly edged into behaving with cold formality when she knew him to be profoundly romantic.

"I'd better go," said Jean-Pierre, waiting for her to come

over to him, but the movement was wanting. "Why don't you come over and kiss me good-bye?"

"You're thinking it was a mistake to come and that's not easy to bear, darling."

"You don't laugh as much as you used to. Does Thomas make life fun for you at all?"

"Oh yes. We catch it on the wing if we're fortunate." She paused. "There's too much we can't tell each other, or don't, him and me."

"Is that the root of why you seem sad?"

"I'm sad—no, moved—you should ask."

"Then is it about us? You would always be sad to believe that a hand had been thrown in."

She thought, and tried carefully to tell the truth. "You're going away. We're not in agreement. We haven't got a country."

Jean-Pierre got up then and went to the door. "Couldn't you tell yourself it's only for a time, like a voyage?"

He kissed her on the forehead and picked up his briefcase without looking back from the door. Catherine watched him from the upper window. He went on foot. She wondered if he were having to work incognito. No. His driver was there, far away, waiting for him. He made no move toward Jean-Pierre, who walked all the way to him. Only then did the man take his briefcase from him and lead Jean-Pierre round a corner where she knew there were steep steps before the first feasible place where a car could have been left.

11

♦

WHEN the news of the bombing of Pearl Harbor came it was eleven o'clock at night in Istanbul. Thomas was taking a break from a long evening at the bank at Istanbul's nearest likeness to New York's Racquet Club. The shortwave wireless was on. The club members, all American, sat closely grouped straining to hear. How much of the fleet had gone? How many deaths? The sound came and went. Somebody at once tried to telephone America but the line was already clogged.

Thomas stood throughout, and more and more of the others came to their feet. Unbearable to idle. Thoughts thrummed. Invasion was something that happened in Europe. America was strong. Unthinkable that the Japanese might invade at any minute. But suddenly, altogether possible.

When the news bulletin ended, people talked in low voices to each other. Of their children. Of cables, diplomatic pouches, any way to communicate. Nationality overcame everything else. Looking out into the dark of Turkey, Thomas wondered if children were being evacuated to Canada. But that would be still less safe. Safety lay nowhere in this no-place with a seven-hour time lag. His eyesight turned inward to see, not Turkey's tranquil darkness with white flowers glowing by moonlight, but the afternoon light of Virginia where his parents were perhaps having tea in the garden with the wireless on the table. He shut his eyes to see America more clearly.

A rabid isolationist, scared enough by the news to take shelter in treating it as a personal political affront, shouted at Thomas, "Now that war's declared you must be pleased as punch."

"*What?*"

"You've always been Roosevelt's man. Japanese must be in F.D.R.'s pay." Thomas turned away. The man shouted to the room in general, voice shaking with bottled fear, "Perfectly well-educated Harvard alumnus. Must be either pinko like Roosevelt or crazy."

Thomas, for his part, no longer gave a fig for the tiny colony that the Racquet Club represented, and could think only of his family, of affairs at the bank, of what was happening to the balance of the dollar; and, in some other part of his mind, of Catherine and of the way the news would surely bridge the gap of incomprehension that sometimes lay between them. He had never met anyone so lucid, so cleared of agitation, but so thoroughly involved in something private.

After snatched sleep at his unused villa, Thomas tried work, but in the crisis all dealing had halted, with the excuse that local time was too far ahead of the New York stock exchange and the bank's Manhattan headquarters. Most of the Americans at the bank here were trying in frenzy to get through to their families, but the lines were endlessly blocked. Cables were being sent by the bank's official method to be passed on, people hoped, to private addresses. The Turkish employees' attitude was gently noncommittal, though his Turkish-born old-American secretary ("Turkish by Caesarean accident," she habitually said) gave him en-

couragement in what she took to be a plight for anyone of
Founding Father ancestry.

"Yes, of course it's devastating", he said. "But also,
terrible as it is, a way to bring about just the involvement
we're duty-bound to have."

"That's the reaction I'd have expected of you, I guess",
she said, "but the Turkish side of me, that's to say the
Caesarean side, has always said to my Pilgrim side that one
mustn't be partisan about this European war."

"Neutrals respecting neutrals" while cheering the most
partisan *Mayflower*.

"Yes," she said.

"No comment can turn into limbo," he said, thinking
also of himself with Catherine, "and no commitment is for
the birds."

"Aye aye, sir," she said, saluting. "I always wanted to be
in the navy."

"Secreting ambitions to take dictation from an admiral?"

"I'd rather *be* an admiral, Mr. Drake," she said, not
laughing at all.

"As you've got dual citizenship I'm sure you could get
yourself into the Waves. You are a surprise. It's terrific."

"The Waves?"

"The women's part of the navy."

"No thanks. Not if it still means taking dictation. I mean
the real navy. All those suffragettes' battles didn't achieve
much."

"You got the vote after the last war because women had
done a lot in munitions."

She let out a scream.

"Admirals don't scream," he said. "I must sprint."

"Bankers don't sprint. Their chauffeurs press the accel-
erator," she said.

She knew where he was going as well as he did. They both had, uncommunicated, a vision of a limousine bumping up and down the steps of the way to Catherine's house, though in her vision the chauffeur was a woman in a cap precisely like an admiral's. Dreams tend to be victorious if dreamed in daylight and with exactitude, she thought, studying a book on naval strategy that she kept in her bottom drawer where other secretaries kept nail polish and oversweet scented soap in flower-decorated soap dishes.

He ran to Catherine's house, holding in his head a daydream of her getting ready the *vitello tonnato* spoken of long ago, though it was only thirty-six hours. She would have forgotten about it. And why should the promise be kept tonight, anyway. Whatever *vitello tonnato* might be.

She turned out to have cooked it. Cold rolls of veal with some cold sauce of pounded tuna fish and mayonnaise.

"There's a certain amount of debris," she said, describing the obvious. Mortar and pestle, frying pan in the sink, the paraphernalia of French mayonnaise, a bin full of eggshells and tuna tins. "The clearing-up's nearly done," she said, giving rise to wonderment in him about how much there had been before.

"It looks delicious," he said.

"No, that's a birthday cake that wouldn't rise for Agnès. She's seventeen and I gave them the day off. It's disgusting. Try it."

Only Catherine, he thought. "It's not as bad as all that," he said. "But isn't the carrot in a carrot cake supposed to be cooked? The carrots shouldn't be sticking up like candles, should they?"

"None of us had ever had it. They liked the sound of the ingredients. Well, I can start again and make a meringue. That's easy."

Alarmed by her aplomb, he said nervously, "I should fall

back on Turkish delight from a packet. Where's the plate that's for us, then?"

"The major cause of the demolition you see is in the fridge."

The dish expressed the mood of cool and calm he had supposed proper to *vitello tonnato* cooked by Catherine. "I'll sprinkle the capers on it and you take up a tray of wine and glasses."

"And paper napkins."

"I'm afraid they'll have to be linen."

"Darling, America's declaring war," he said.

"I know." She hesitated. "The shortwave wireless. That's why I'm late. Are you okay?"

"About time." There was no question that he looked buoyant.

"I thought you might have very mixed feelings. And that that was why you dwelt on paper napkins. So to speak."

He swung her up into his arms and kissed her, and then went upstairs to the room where they were to have dinner. He found traces of someone having been there. Two people had been playing draughts. There was a tray with two emptied glasses and a half-full bottle of Marc.

"What's up?" she said, coming in with yet another tray.

"Too many events."

"Pearl Harbour and—"

"Tell me the truth."

"Yes."

"Has Jean-Pierre been here?"

"Yes."

"Does he come often?"

"It's the first time for a very long time." She went on standing there, in stasis, with the tray in her hands.

"How much did it mean to you?"

She had trouble answering honestly. "A good deal," was the best she could manage at first.

"Did he ask about me?"

"Yes."

"Didn't he mind?"

"He wasn't going to say so. We really are a very long way apart."

Both of them now seemed stalemated. She said, absurdly as she heard the words, "There was nothing to hide from you so I left the tray and didn't plump the cushions."

"If I roll my eyes, which is what they seem to be doing of their own accord this evening anyway, I can see at least ten trays in this room," he said. "Used and unused." He went around to the side of the bed, and said, "Darling, this is our breakfast tray from yesterday. The exquisite woman isn't a furtive slob, is she? And didn't Jean-Pierre notice? Or if he did, didn't he mind? I can tell it's our breakfast tray because of the remnants of my runny egg yolk."

"Yes, I expect so, to the first two questions, and no, I don't think so at all, to the third." She paused. "I said yes to one question that I've forgotten but I think it was something about my being a slob. Yes, I may be. The excuses were, are Jean-Pierre, Pearl Harbor, the girls' being off, failed carrot cake, in no particular order."

His thoughts for once switched away from Catherine to be waylaid by the fortune-teller who so plausibly blended with this mined new landscape.

"And as we all know, two excuses are deadeningly laborious. I don't know if four is so far above the average that it cancels out and becomes meticulous."

She waited, then went on.

"There's even one more. It's to do with Ann Wisner. That excuse I just can't make."

"To protect her?" Thomas said.

"I truly can't say."

She carried out two trays in turn. He shuddered as both of them went, once at the remnants of festivity he didn't care to imagine with Jean-Pierre, once at the spooned-out cold egg yolk on his own plate. All over America parents' stomachs were heaving at what their sons were going to have to face with the War upon them. Here in Istanbul, his stomach was heaving at a leftover egg yolk that occupied Europe would have valued like a long-lost and by now forgotten trinket.

He tried to get through a large helping of *vitello tonnato*, sitting opposite her on their cushions in the usual position, with the tray on the floor between them. To her relief, he seemed to enjoy the strange combination. "Neither fish, flesh, nor fowl", he said.

"Fish and flesh, but the saving grace of no runny egg yolks."

He suddenly looked as if he were trying not to gag. Pearl Harbor, of course. (Combined with a struggle with the veal?)

She touched his hand with a forkful of the food on it. "Don't have it if you don't like it."

He twisted his head away. "Overemotion." Then it was Pearl Harbor. "I'm sorry," he went on. "It was also the effort you went to for us."

As they went toward bed, he thought over weightily about the notebook and knew it. But Hilda's insistence held out too much promise of an end to his ache about Catherine's straits for him easily to put it by. In the way of things, the insistence gained force as darkness grew. Hilda's noxious character was so far from the sane that he began to believe her to be right in finding him grieved even when he was brilliantly happy. Being herself amoral, she could cast others into a purgatory where they could not quite control what they were thinking. On his own, he by instinct now gave Catherine leeway. He had found latent in him her own characteristic of leaving people room. But with this figment of Hilda hanging there in his head, an unruly part of his mind pestered Catherine with unspoken suspicions without his knowing that he was not their author. Hilda had made of him a tool, turning into an ignoble agent a man of resolve and amplitude.

He thought that, by listening to Catherine's lucid voice and listening to the shortwave wireless news in her bedroom with her, all thoughts of Hilda had been banished. But as soon as he left the room to have a bath, he found himself imagining the bedroom with her gone from it and he alone, watching for intruders as he looked for her notebook. The hell with the capacity of our species for endless rehearsal, far worse than its opposite of endless reenactment.

12

♦

THOMAS woke again and
again in the night, and then slept without moving until after
nine. Catherine woke him by coming in with another tray.
"Coffee and croissants and figs and tinned orange juice," she
said, putting the tray down on a carpet-covered orange
cushion and slopping the coffee a little.

"Try the floor. It's flatter," he said, holding his knees to
his chest and clutching them. The movement was so painful
that she thought he might have appendicitis and came round
the side of the pile of huge cushions that was their bed. She
held a hand to his forehead. "You might have a temperature," she said.

"Not according to my watch," he said. "Hold on a
second."

As if that wasn't what she was doing, of course.

"I didn't do us any eggs today," she said, hoping to
relieve the pain he was in.

"Oh, thank you," he said in all earnest, writhing on his
side, clasping his toes and pulling them up as far as possible.

"Can you describe what's hurting so much?"

"Cramp," he said between gasps. "*Both* calves." He
rolled off the cushions and stood, hanging on to her armoire

as he lifted himself up and down on the balls of his feet. "It's okay, it's loosening."

"It looks agonizing."

"Didn't you ever have it?"

"Not from the look of it."

He went on flexing his calf muscles. "One's getting unknotted. No, they're both getting worse now. Would you rub very hard? Both calves. No, much harder, and that's the wrong place. Four inches lower. Yes, there. You must be able to feel the place."

After minutes of violent rubbing by Catherine he collapsed back on the bed, again grasping his toes and pulling them upward.

"Is it still just as bad?" she said.

"It's okay now. This is just to stop it happening again."

"What exactly is it?"

"Cramp. Muscle cramp. All athletes get it sometimes. You have to force yourself to move the muscles. They go into spasm. They get into a knot."

"It looks appallingly painful."

"It's like being hit on the back of the calf very hard with an ace serve if you're playing doubles and standing at the net playing with a terrific partner. It can also happen if you're swimming in a relay race. It happened to me once just at the turn. Of course then it's worse because you're letting the whole team down. The cold water adds to it."

"Good Lord."

"You just have to pack it in and somehow get through with one leg. And then of course with the strain on that leg, the one that's left, it's likely to go too and then all you can do is butterfly back-crawl with your arms, holding your knees up to your chest."

"Heavens."

"You lose seconds every lap."

"Doesn't anyone want you to stop?"

"One can't stop."

"Because of the pain?"

"No, one simply shouldn't."

She poured some coffee and pushed his right toes upward with one hand while she held the cup to his mouth with the other.

"I can't drink sideways," he said. "Put the cup down and prop pillows behind my head." She did as she was told and he swallowed a hot cupful. "Now hold the cup against the right calf. There's nothing like heat. No, it's tepid already."

She ran down to the kitchen and boiled some water and put it into a bowl, reminding herself of every bad film she had ever seen with a childbirth scene in it, though she had never known what the boiling water was for. Not for sterilizing surgical instruments, surely, because the water wouldn't still be boiling, and not possibly to dunk the baby in. Françoise and Agnès, watching, made the same connection and were mystified.

"Have we got some cloths for me to wring out in this?" said Catherine. Cloths were produced. "Mr. Drake's got very bad cramp. At least it has been bad and it might be again."

"You didn't slop any of it, did you?" said Thomas as she came in with the steaming bowl. "A hot-water bottle might have been better. Or a heating pad. Even liniment."

"We haven't got a hot-water bottle or heating pad. Or liniment."

"Thank heaven you didn't slop the water, then. This house probably hasn't a thing in it for a second-degree burn. It would have been at least second-degree if you'd slipped and the water had been near boiling."

"How's the cramp?"

"Completely gone. We'll have a croissant, shall we?"

The crisis might never have happened. Catherine remained in ignorance, though guilty about a house with no hot-water bottle, no heating pad, no liniment. Thomas clung to his memory of pain to forget the nightmare that had caused it. He had been woken suddenly by a cramp caused by having dreamed of running very fast from Catherine's house, where he had been crouched on his knees looking for her Paisley notebook, to Hilda's little house in the pathways. He played back his resulting fuss with loathing.

"Thank you for putting up with that," he said. "I behaved horribly."

"You were in pain. I didn't know what to do."

Catherine and he finished breakfast in silence. She went out quickly, kissing him good-bye and saying that she would be back soon with news from America through a better shortwave wireless than hers. It didn't seem enough information. What was she shielding? Or whom? She sometimes left gaps that she would ordinarily fill in. Look at the easy fondness for Jean-Pierre that she communicated.

She had left her wicker basket behind, with the flap open. There was a crumpled piece of paper in it with the cobbler's address heading, amateurishly printed, and rows of letters and marks that he took to be mnemonics, though he could make nothing of them. The fact that she had crumpled the piece of paper with the obvious intent of throwing it away later made him fearful for her. He turned aside from snooping once he had recognized her handwriting in the unfamiliar notes and again rehearsed the visit to Hilda that he was going to make himself carry through. But this time it was reenactment that smote, not rehearsal. He played through their duologue again and again. Memory, the long arm of blight. How dare she implant in him fear for Catherine when his beloved girl was so peerlessly beyond it?

The engine of his mind was idling. If only she would

come back, there would be no impulse left in him to go to Hilda. For all his effort not to pry even in thought, he found her sudden determined absence disconcerting. Uppermost was the horror that she was perhaps being blackmailed by some anti-Fascist fanatic in Turkey because of her vulnerable place as the solitary wife of a Vichy diplomat he understood to be rigid to the point of ruthlessness. She was obviously at odds with everything he stood for, though she was not the woman to say so in public. He forgot that the idea of Jean-Pierre as rigid and ruthless had come from Hilda, never from Catherine. Loathing of Jean-Pierre's chauffeur was the most that she allowed herself.

Over their bed of brilliant huge cushions there was a facsimile page, framed, with a sentence ringed round. "He has a lifelong love for politics, though a lifelong scorn for the people who practice them." Had she thought that? Of someone she admired? If not, whom was she quoting? About whom? Was she describing Jean-Pierre? It sounded very much like a description of a diplomat's views. Then he puzzled some more, and realized that it could well be applied to any political satirist, any political cartoonist. He looked round at her room. The books on her bookcases: rows of those yellow paperbacks in French that he had never explored, a book about de Gaulle where the quote he had seen was marked, books by Melville and Burke and Disraeli, a whole row of Swift and his biographers, Balzac, Kafka, Evelyn Waugh, Jane Austen, Gibbon's *Decline and Fall* (read, he found, every volume of it, with slips of paper sticking out between some of the pages), A. A. Milne. Beside the A. A. Milne there was a glass pot with a wooden top half full of scraps of paper. The scraps were little notes in a writing he didn't recognize, until he saw at the bottom of the pot a photograph of two children dressed alike in a country garden. One of the children was perhaps five, writing at a table, and the other no more than two and a half, watching with her back to the camera. The watcher had the small plump elbow of a toddler and was only just tall enough to prop it on the table. The caption to the photograph was printed in the same handwriting as the slips of paper, an older child's writing: "Me and Catherine at Grandmère's in Grasse." One of the scraps of paper inside that showed through the glass said, "A useful pot to put things in, for Catherine from Emma forever."

The rest of the room, when he looked at it alone, spoke so much of Catherine's adult life that the treasure pot of her childhood was startling to come upon. He looked again at a childhood notebook in his hands and found, near the beginning, a page where a copper beech leaf and a flower petal had been dried and pasted in long ago, with a big spotted feather curling over them. Hilda, *no;* hold *off;* odious of him to have explored the privacy of Catherine's past without her knowledge. He set out for the bank to put some normality into the day, which had turned chilly. His mind went back to the doors of the bedroom, shut tightly behind brilliant yellow curtains edged with gold braid, drawn back every morning by Catherine when their breakfast came and fastened with brass lions' heads that she had once told him she had found in Venice. She had been to Venice on honeymoon. He knew that through Hilda. He could make out the palaces and churches in the background of the photograph she had from a set of labeled engravings on the walls of the bedroom he had just left. No, quit puzzling, he said to himself. Catherine is clarity. The essence of her is whatever she's up to, with her Paisley notebook and her knowledge of music: she's in control of it. She's beyond us, far ahead of us, and doesn't even know it. So much doesn't know it that we can leave things to her, follow her without ever feeling behind, cross my heart and hope to die.

When he arrived at the bank, he found that it was closed in honor of Turkey's national holiday. The mood in the streets outside was exasperatingly festive. Why hadn't his secretary told him? An Englishwoman he knew from the British Council, Mary Heron, a client too, was standing outside the bank shaking the huge doorknobs uselessly. "Can you open it up?" she said to him.

"I'm as stalemated as you are."

"I should have expected you all to be frightfully busy, just having joined the War."

She talked as if it were a question of making up four at bridge.

"It seems to be a holiday," he said.

"A Turkish holiday, not an American bank's holiday."

"Banks observe the customs of the countries they're based in."

"But I needed lots of small change for our garden party. Haven't you got the keys?"

He shook his head.

"You're a high-up, though, aren't you?" she said. "I mean, you don't stand behind a counter. You sit. That reminds me, I'd completely forgotten my chairs. Where can I hire at least twelve dozen little gold chairs? Parents will want to watch the sports. Then we're doing Gilbert and Sullivan."

"Has Istanbul ever been exposed to Gilbert and Sullivan?"

"Our Turkish friends have been rehearsing and rehearsing. They're tremendously keen. A *moment musicale* in time of war. I should know what they are celebrating, shouldn't I?

One doesn't like being ignorant. Aren't I lacking. Do brief me. Your diary will tell you."

"It's at the bank."

"Oh well. There'll be someone I can ask tactfully. The council's representative himself planned the whole thing, the British vice-consul is joining in, and of course the name of the holiday is on all our interoffice memos." She pronounced the word "meemos". She rattled onward. "The meaning of the date has just slipped my mind, which is entirely filled with music and the gilt chairs."

Thomas felt as if he were having a nightmare with his feet stuck in mud. He would never be able to leave, never catch up.

"I think you'd better come with me. Naughty man, I'm going to tell the council that it's all your fault if there are repercussions. Nothing must go awry. We absolutely relied on an American bank to be open for our festivities, and as a thank-you present for the help you're going to give me—the council's this way—" (she had been leading him in her wake, holding on to his elbow, now turning him to the left and up a new row of steps) "—as a thank-you present we should be honored to have you at the sports and the Gilbert and Sullivan."

"Which Gilbert and Sullivan?" he asked, far beyond asking her whether this was the best choice in English composers.

"*Trial by Jury*. The council's representative is aflame with interest in G. and S. And he simply knows the Turkish mind backward. He did either *HMS Pinafore* or *The Pirates of Penzance* last year or the year before, I can't for the life of me remember which year was which, but anyway it came off with tremendous success. Those years we had more time for details of admin., what I call the kitchen of life, but Pearl

Harbor put everything like visits to the bank absolutely out of our minds."

Eventually the problem of the gilt chairs was solved by the British Council representative himself. "People and parents can simply stand on their two game feet to watch the three-legged race, the ginger-beer drinking race, and the greasy pole contest." Much eagerness was in the air. "Indeed," he said, a spidery figure in a black suit who looked more like a Victorian ledger-keeper than an arm of international understanding in the arts, "some of us grown-ups may well want to participate. And we shall be sitting down in our pride and joy of a theater for the Gilbert and Sullivan, which will revive everyone. And we can pay our various helpmates out of petty cash, so everything is solved, except the two hundred and fifty copies of my little monograph on W. S. Gilbert's gift for collaboration which have not yet arrived. But we still have a few hours to go before the fun. So all will be well."

The monographs arrived after a time of tension, when Thomas had been drawn into making the punch "to while away the waiting." The goal to scold Hilda into sense seemed to be getting further and further away. Turkish people were resting after a dress rehearsal of *Trial by Jury,* lying down on the sofas inside the house in their costumes, which the representative, beaming with excitement, told them to treat like eggshells. The barristers in their gowns were to be particularly careful, and putting on the wigs should be left until "nearer the climax," in case the wig adhesive were not to last out the interim. There was a small Turkish orchestra. The representative was to do the makeup himself.

"It does my heart good to see the representative so enjoying himself," said Mary Heron. "He has so many functions to go to, and so many visitors to look after. All last week we had a most demanding Mistress of the Robes together with a key man from Rolls-Royce airplanes. England is searching everywhere for spare parts that the poor Turks were promised by Germany but the Nazis went back on their word and now it's up to England to find spare parts for German airplanes. Typical. There *is* a war on. This busy man couldn't get a word in edgeways with the Mistress of the Robes around. She wouldn't take no for an answer whatever one did. Rolls-Royce had to walk or go by jeep because she insisted on ladies first and she got the official car. She was only here to present a scholarship sponsored by the Queen. Now where were we."

Thomas made his excuses when her back was turned and ran all the way to Hilda's little street. He went up the stairs but found the top door closed and locked. When he came down again, ever-present Sukru was there, giggling. "She closed. Today holiday," he said. "No mail."

Thomas found himself saying, as if the boy had enough English to catch tired emphases, "There *is* a war on." Mary Heron's commonplaces were very catching. "A fortune-teller shouldn't take a holiday when men's lives are at stake." He had nowhere in particular that he wanted to go. He couldn't go back to Catherine's house until he had seen Hilda and scotched her. "Where's the fortune-teller?" he asked many a passerby, and most of them looked at him as if he were more than a little mad to be so frenzied. Some of them tried helpfully to show in sign language that there were fortune-tellers by the score outside the ramparts of the old city, but he insistently pointed upward to the sign over her door. Surely hers should be a twenty-four-hour job. He traveled up and down street after street in search of her, foolishly, and then went to the bank's flat for an hour or two to be alone. There were no books there, only English-language newspapers carefully folded, dating from the time when he had first come to the wretched place. The bed was unmade: clearly the manservant still put in an appearance every day to merit his wages, but used the villa now as his home. The manservant's linen and cotton clothes, laundered—no doubt at the bank's expense—were in the wardrobe. Even here, in this hireling of a home, he had become an intruder. He left again as noisily as possible to establish ownership, though there was no one to hear him, and went to the British Council again. The three-legged race was in full swing. Turkish parents had indeed joined in this strange race in which pairs of people wriggled a right and a left leg apiece into a sack and tried to run to a winning post. The representative was in charge of the whistle and the vice-consul was referee. The greasy pole was yet to come. He saw Mary Heron, who exclaimed, "Where did you disappear to?"

"A minor errand."

"You could have helped with greasing the pole. It really is a job for two. I couldn't for the life of me remember how to do it. It's been such ages. One rubbed it with soap, I thought, and then I wondered whether oil of some kind didn't enter into it. So there is a little of both on the pole and my hands are *redolent*." She said the word as though she were spelling it. "A mixture of olive oil and that pervasive Turkish flower fragrance that smells so very little of flowers. They do put it on everything. One wonders all one's life what attar of roses is, doesn't one. One of those things one always means to look up. And every time one does, one forgets it again, like the date of the Assumption of the B.V.M."

"A make of car?"

She looked embarrassed and said, "Oh dear. I'm treading on toes, aren't I. Heavens alive, and I'm the British Council. We really don't think we rule the waves, you know, but with an Established Church one does forget that there are others. I really am frightfully sorry. I'd never have said such a thing to a Muslim. Probably you're not even a *nonpracticing* Anglican. B.V.M. is for the Blessed Virgin Mary. Now I wonder if you'd be a hero and make sure we've bedded down the greasy pole properly."

A pair of Istanbul identical twins, aged seven and a half, made a popular win at the three-legged race. The representative had raced up to the winning post with his whistle to help the vice-consul if there should be an argument about a tie. The greasy pole, newly introduced to Turkey, led to hilarity or total lack of comprehension. Eventually the representative ran into the house and came back in a pair of tennis shorts with no shoes on. "The thing is," he said, not yet having mastered Turkish: the vice-consul translated for him, phrase by phrase, "to grip the pole as hard as possible with the naked feed crossed behind one and lug oneself up six inches at a time, first by the legs, then by the hands. Never both at the same time. And if one slips below the slope of the pole, don't let go. With luck and stamina one can hold fast and sort of wriggle around into the topmost position again. Or continue the attempt on Everest while hanging from below, of course"— he said, incidentally swiveling round by accident at just this point in the demonstration—"as I said, hanging from below, which puts a great deal of strain on the limbs. One does it like a monkey," he ended, sliding and slipping and somehow gaining an inch at a time. The endeavor and its victory seemed crucial, and when he made it to the top of the pole there was a great deal of clapping.

The field was then open to the visitors. Most of them were in garden-party clothes, the women with wide-brimmed hats. A number of Istanbul's street urchins were there, too, who would have been natural greasy-pole climbers. They hung back. The daughter of the American ambassador won against few comers. Thomas, squash player or no, was not going to try. He already smelled enough of the olive oil and flowered-soap mixture that had come off onto him during the bedding of the pole.

Suddenly he saw Hilda's long sad face. In her normal clothes, not the norm of others, she looked more than ever like one of the Bloomsbury group. She was dressed in long gray muslin, shoes with little Edwardian heels and silver buckles, earrings that this time seemed real, a big gray straw hat. No makeup, her face peculiarly pallid, her eyes so like Virginia Woolf's that he narrowly stopped himself from talking to her about *Orlando*. She seemed to have been watching him for quite a time.

For lack of anything else to do, he waved at her.

The British representative, who had been shepherding people to refreshments (punch, lettuce sandwiches, chocolate biscuits), disappeared into the house to start his make-up job with his singers. As he left he waved at Thomas, who waved back. Hilda also waved. The representative walked fast, singing, "He'll tell us how he came to be a judge."

"I said we should meet again," said Hilda, coming over to Thomas.

Thomas said, flustered, "You were shut," as if he needed to apologize for an unkept appointment.

"This is a local holiday," she said.

"Could you do a little work?" he said. How to put such a thing. Had he a ten-dollar bill on him? But one could hardly pay her openly here. What guise did she present to the British vice-consul?

Reading his mind eerily, she said, "The vice-consul and I have a common interest in the restoration of Byzantine icons. As to your question, it will be possible to see you in an hour at my own house. That is to say, if you have the notebook. Otherwise there is no help I can give you."

He shook his head. How odd. She didn't believe him. She laughed without any movement of the face and said, "You would be a very bad spy."

*I*n an hour promptly he was at her now-open door, and she was at her table as if nothing had moved since her last meeting. The blinds were drawn, the lamp and its red fringed lampshade gave the room a glow of banal warmth. She had changed into her fortune-teller's garb, changed her earrings, slashed red lipstick onto her lips. Even the child was still there as if she had never moved, clambering about the room in a pristine white dress eating a sandwich from a supply that she had tucked into the secret pocket of her petticoat. He recognized lettuce sandwiches. Surely nowhere else but at the British Council were lettuce sandwiches considered celebratory today. The child soberly offered him one, and he soberly ate. Sugar dusting from a Turkish sweetmeat was clinging to it, and other edible pocket remnants. Whose child?

"Is she your daughter?" he said to Hilda.

"The child was at the garden party. You didn't notice her," said Hilda, casting the point aside as usual. "You have brought the notebook?" for a second time.

"No."

"That puts us at a disadvantage." She said something in Turkish to the child, who clambered obediently out of a bottom drawer where she had chosen to sit and waited at the door for a moment of counting her sandwiches before going down the stairs.

"Do you let her go into the streets by herself? She can't be more than three," said Thomas.

"What we have to say is not for her ears. Now, you must concentrate. Put your hand on mine. No, the left one, palm upward."

His gorge rose as usual at the foibles of her trade. "Can't we do it without the theatrical nonsense?"

"You should cooperate. It will be important to you. You have ten dollars?"

"Yes, but I can give it to you when we've finished."

"Now. It is necessary." She put her free hand to her forehead. "For the rhythm of insight to flow."

"Everything's to do with money."

"This is true. You're in money yourself. A major part of the story in which you are playing has to do with this subject."

"There's also loyalty. And worth." Talisman words so that he would hold his own. "A world outside."

"The money."

He passed it. She tucked the note under an unpleasant green jade frog among the objects on the table.

"To help you, I must know what you hope."

"What?"

"I must know your own greatest wishes." He suddenly thought he heard a Norwegian accent. A Quisling or loyal? Keep away from the subject of Germany. "I just hope she's all right."

"You detect things that are threatening."

"She's brave, you see. She may be at risk."

"To do with France, my cards tell me."

"Bullshit."

"The cards do not lie."

He would give her another test, though the folly and the artful ignorance he was getting from her now were overwhelming. "Vichy? Or the Maquis?"

"You are harboring hatred of my knowledge. It means that the messages in the cards spell mistrust. I see confusion in them, confusion for you everywhere, because you are mistrustful. I see a jumble here. Yes, an urgent message that no cipher clerk could understand."

"Don't tell me you know one."

She held her silence.

"Probably one of your clients," he said. "You're such a born-looking conspirator that no one would dream of suspecting you."

"I practice an ancient art."

"*Art?* Soothsayers are on a level with barber-surgeons." He felt furious about her dizzy games with constancy and love. A lifetime's loathing of superstition and pretences of black magic's potency made him look at her at last with a sense of humor and a sense of the sane. "Blame it on being a foreigner," he said out loud by mistake, and found as she heard the words that she had no idea what he meant. So much for her sham mind-reading. He got up, shook hands, told her that she would do well to get a bulb with higher wattage, and went quickly to the door. Sukru, who knew every trick of an Arab street runner but made extraordinarily little in bribes because it was clear to everyone that he was merely working for any covert enterprise in Istanbul, came upstairs with the child. She had been on Thomas's mind as much as the copied notes when he clambered back up to the room. The boy asked in Turkish for some piastres for looking after the child. The meaning of his sentence was clear enough without language. Thomas found ten piastres and a piece of chewing gum. When he left, after tossing and catching the elated little girl above his head, he had forgotten Hilda's force. She didn't matter, he thought. Hold on to the commonplace. As soon as the sound of his footsteps had drained away, Hilda put the ten-dollar bill into a secret drawer in a miniature Chinese writing table, gave the boy a single piastre and told him to take her notes of every one of Thomas's questions to a cipher clerk who indeed used the cover of being a simpleminded regular customer. She herself was not simpleminded at all, nor was the clerk. Both had a phobic insistence on inhuman detail. Lacking a sense of measure, they were ready employees of fanaticism.

13

♦

CATHERINE was urgently on her way to Ann Wisner's again. She was stopped by a cheerful wave from the urchin Sukru. He shifted importantly through his letters and papers—among them the scraps for the cipher clerk that Hilda had entrusted to him, which he was considering throwing away because she had not given him what he regarded as the going rate—and said in Turkish, "Nothing for you today, but a pile for Mr. Thomas Drake."

He handed the pile over, leaving himself with only the scraps of paper. Catherine gave him five piastres and some French honey that was wrapped for him in the wicker basket, ready for their next daily meeting. The meeting was never arranged: he simply appeared. Istanbul was like that. She noticed the papers that were left, and said, "Are those for us too?"

"No, somebody else. She gave me one piastre to deliver them which is not enough. I'm very busy."

Catherine dreaded the thought that somebody was not going to get something vital to them, and said, "I think it would be best to deliver them quickly, don't you? Because of your reputation. And think of it. They might be love letters." She gave him a few more piastres to make up for what he regarded as underpayment, and that did the trick, along with her mention of love letters, which spoke to his lonesome circumstances. Greatly cheered to think of himself as a courier who might be bringing about a consummation of some romance of mythic sweep, he ran Hilda's errand subsidized by Catherine's reading of his love-parched nature as well as by her piastres.

Catherine had vital work to do at Ann's. But when she had opened her wicker basket for the honey, she had seen a formal lunch invitation for this Turkish celebration day that she had completely forgotten about, though she had put the invitation there yesterday as a reminder. Cursing herself, she tried to make the visit as fast as possible. Most people seemed to have nothing to do but gossip over martinis. The small talk was hard to participate in amiably. There was much Anglo-American debate of the quickest way to get from Ankara to Istanbul. The women deferred to the men. Some swore by the train, careful to honor the national pride of the Turks present on their celebratory day. The Turks, in honor of the many non-Turkish friends present, themselves criticized the crowds on the train, the lack of upkeep, the lateness. An American attaché stood up for the punctuality of the dawn train. There was much complimentary laughter about Americans' capacities as early-morning risers. "Another martini for the road to the dining room," called the British press attaché, looking around the room for journalists to support him. "There don't seem to be any journalists here," he said to Catherine.

"I expect they're filing stories," she said.

"Yes, that would be the answer, no doubt," he said.

Though a windy man, who tried to correct the impression he gave by walking very fast, he had once been a member of the press himself, as he told everyone. He had worked for three months on the house journal of the London Electricity Board before he was sacked for idleness and went to university, where he had taken a third. The L.E.B. job did not appear in his entry in *Who's Who*, but the experience gave him a wonderful ease in speaking about deadlines. He was seated next to Catherine at lunch: four courses, to be followed by Turkish coffee on the terrace. They discussed the time difference between Istanbul and London, Istanbul and New York, Istanbul and Los Angeles.

"It must be a frightful strain for foreign correspondents," he said.

"Yes, it must," she said, thinking of the time in Paris.

"Living in so many time zones," he said.

"Yes indeed."

"How lucky one is being based all in one spot."

"Yes." She ate some bread. "All? I'm sorry. You mean all of us at this table?"

"No, all of the self. The body and the mind and so on of oneself being all together. In a cluster, so to speak."

"I know what you mean," she said, her mind on getting to the shortwave radio.

Coffee was announced.

"I'll do the honors," he said, grasping her cup and his own.

"I really should be going," she said, looking at her watch.

"Our hostess will be mortally offended. On the national holiday," he said.

*S*o she followed him to the terrace. He tripped on a step between the dining room and the terrace and, in the effort to catch him before he hurt himself, Catherine found that the heel had come off her right shoe.

"Miracle of miracles, our coffee is still intact. I used my arms and hands as a sort of gimbal in the storm, to borrow an image from 'Those in peril on the sea,' " he said, humming. "It's my favorite hymn. Isn't it yours? 'For those in peril on the sea.' Dum dum dum, dum dum, dum dum, dum. I've forgotten the rest of the words."

" 'Oh hear us when we cry to Thee, For those in peril on the sea' is the way it ends," she said. " 'Eternal Father, strong to save, Whose arm doth bind the restless wave, Oh hear us when we cry to thee,' " she sang, "oh damn."

"I was saying 'dum.' Aren't you brill."

"Brill?"

"Brilliant."

"I said 'damn.' I've bust my shoe heel."

"My dear *lady*," he said, standing there with the cups in his hands. "What will you do." He paused. "I'd carry you to a chair but I've got these cups and there isn't a table."

"Or a chair," said Catherine. "We're obviously supposed to stand for the coffee. Speeds things."

There was consternation. It spread. As she fled on her bare feet there were many offers of pairs of shoes from her hostess. "Except that I've got these wide feet, real moon-man feet, and yours are so *narrow*." Many of the women discussed the difficulty of the narrowness of their own particular feet, the impossibility of getting what one wanted in an A fitting, let alone a double A, and of course a triple A (as darling Catherine's size must be) would be out of the question except in wonderful Istanbul where cobblers do miracles with any sort of foot-last, however aristocratically narrow, for practically nothing. By this time Catherine was half a mile onward, running on the bare feet that she preferred anyway, and finding the cobbler where she had last done currency conversion.

He was open. He was quite amazed to find that his advertised services were needed, rather than the currency converting that Catherine usually came to him for. He had stayed open for her especially, he said, because he knew she would be wanting to give presents to her servants today of all days. And that this holiday might well have slipped her mind, her mind being so busy. As he spoke, he mended her heel perfectly, and she was off to the British Council where the sports were in full swing to make her apologies for not being able to come to *Trial by Jury* and to ask their kindness in letting her use their telephone line.

"It's my godchild's birthday. I'll be calling a great friend on the *Wall Street Journal* who's the child's father," she said.

The secretary of the representative was a friend who had known her in Paris. "It'll be terribly hard raising the operator today, I'm afraid."

"I should have a go, if I may. I'll get the time and the cost and pay you back. Thank-you a lot. The child's six and she'll be in her father's office. He said he was going to give her a four-ice-cream lunch at his desk."

"Of course. One has to cope with the time difference," said the secretary. Again.

Catherine seemed to exercise some sort of magic over intractable telephones. Jean-Pierre had once remarked on it. "I think it must be because you don't lose your temper." She remembered that as she tried this time. Heel mended, celebratory day, concentrate on people in Istanbul. "Keep the mind active and the body seated." Who said that? Some wise old man. She thought of it as she sat on the edge of a sofa in the representative's study. She sat down on the sofa properly. As soon as she did an operator answered. She got through to the child in New York in four minutes. They had been writing notes to each other that started with a single letter: a letter added to in turn by each of them to make as long a word as possible. The person who put on the last addable-to-letter won. The last letter from the child had got as far as "gard." Catherine gave her the "E" on the telephone.

"I know, I know. 'N.'"

"You've won." Gardener, gardening: no, not at her age, not on the overseas telephone. "Have you had your birthday cake yet?"

"Ages ago. Ages and ages."

And so on.

Then she spoke to the child's father, an old friend, who rapidly gave her some figures from the *Wall Street Journal* without wasting time on identifying the commodities they referred to because the two of them had long since established the order. She wrote the figures down fast, though she was remembering them anyway, had a swift exchange of affectionate sentences and put down the receiver, looking at her watch. The operator rang back with the charges, a system new to her that she thought to have been invented by Catherine herself. Catherine found the right number of piastres and took them down to the secretary with a five-pound note.

"It seemed amazingly cheap," he said. "I think the operator made a mistake. Put this fiver in the kitty anyway in case she underestimated."

"Are you going to stay for *Trial by Jury?*" The secretary made a small face and Catherine smiled.

"Has it *been* a trial?"

"Everyone is so bucked about it that it's worth it. Though they're the most maddening tunes. You can't get them out of your head."

"I really am sorry, but I'm horribly late at Ann Wisner's because I broke a shoe heel."

"And no one's open."

"One cobbler I know was."

"Worth a lot more than a day off to him, I should think. I don't suppose he can rely on more than one customer a day. Play me some Mozart or something tomorrow, I'm going nuts with these tunes. We've had thirty-one rehearsals."

As Catherine left, after seeking out the representative's wife, she suddenly saw Thomas's back. He was running out of the entrance gates in the opposite direction to the way to her house. What on earth had brought him here? She, too, assumed that he would be at work, underlined by just having had the *Wall Street Journal* figures reported to her. She had promised to be back fast with news from America. For the only time in her life with Thomas or anyone else, she had to suppress the impulse to run after him and hold him. Ann first. All the same she called out to him as loudly as she could, but he didn't hear. She felt divided from him by glass, as though she were locked on the ground in an airport watching him on the runway steps to leave for somewhere far off. He seemed hell-bent.

*B*y the time she got to Ann's house she had banished the ache for Thomas and only wanted to explain her lateness to Ann as fast as possible. Ann was a jump ahead of her and said, before she had opened her mouth, "Darling, it doesn't matter. You forgot something, that's all. You were supposed to go to a ball and you bust your glass slipper at midnight. Thank God you *are* late. I had to go out because I had to find a telephone to tell Kemal he's forgotten he should be in Ankara."

"Where did you telephone from?"

"The American Consulate."

"I've just been at the British Council using their phone."

"About your glass slipper."

"You really are extraordinary. I did actually bust a shoe heel but the call was about a godchild's birthday. Lordy me, the truth's laborious.

"No it isn't. It's swift."

"The essence of it."

"To be essential, Kemal plundered the diplomatic pouch of someone or other and we've got two Hershey bars, six Cadbury's blended chocolate and an orange," said Ann. Catherine suddenly became reflective.

"Just before Pearl Harbor an American ship marvelously brought England an orange for every single citizen. There hadn't been oranges since the War. And the Germans dropped a direct hit on the London docks that night and they got the cargo of oranges. The crew were on shore leave and not a life was lost. Only oranges." A long pause, charged. Catherine had to walk about to order herself out of that. "Cor, Hershey's *and* Cadbury's."

"Well," said Ann, "the Nazi hit must have been either a tragedy or a miracle."

"Definitely a miracle, but I'm not saying there weren't a lot of pangs. For America to have sent fifty million oranges—"

"Darling Catherine, you're being absurd. You're the bravest woman I've ever known and you're on the point of crying about fifty million oranges."

"A terrific gesture went wrong." Catherine went on walking about. Shake things off. "Yes. Onward."

"If you're under some strain you would tell me?"

"We're well off." Catherine brought her mind back to the figures in her head, and also to Ann. "Your telephone call to Kemal. Was that all right?"

"Fine."

"How long did it take to get him?"

"Two hours."

"He's only two miles away. Why didn't you walk?"

"The operator said the call from the Consulate would get through in a couple of minutes. It went on taking longer and longer. She kept me on the line checking a sum for an earlier call she'd put through that she'd under-charged for and it would have to come out of her own pocket. She said it was going to take a year to pay the Turkish telephone company and they might sack her. I couldn't leave her alone on the other end."

Catherine thought, this is one of the reasons I love Ann. Who but Ann would speak so naturally of not leaving someone alone in straits when the companionship is coming from a stranger over a telephone line. And at the same time, she said out loud, "Oh Lord, that would have been my call. I *thought* it was undercharged. Is there only one telephone operator in all Istanbul?"

"Well, it is a public holiday, and there don't seem to be more than eight telephones in Istanbul."

"Where is the telephone company?" said Catherine.

"Why?"

"Obviously I must find her and pay her."

They both paused. Catherine went on, "I can hear what you're thinking. I'll have to do the wireless first. It may be too late already."

Catherine went to work, her memory focused and sharp. Ann went into the garden in the chill twilight of the Istanbul spring, watered a few bushes in case anyone was spying. Catherine watched her. The reception from the radio was nil without the antennae arranged. She shook her head at Ann and pointed to her own ears. In the distance, perhaps a quarter of a mile away, there was a sudden burst of light. A firework? Then there was another burst, no more than two hundred yards. A firework would make sense on a public holiday, but Catherine mouthed "be careful" to Ann.

"What am I to be careful of?" said Ann out loud, coming in with her watering can.

"There are fireworks going on. Someone's about."

"And?"

"If anyone's watching, they'd see you putting up the radio antennae. That's all. It's just the sort of clue that the dealers in intrigue get paid a mint for."

"Darling, I just look like some very boring wife and gardener. Though Kemal would be pained if he heard me put it like that."

"Does he mind about having this radio about?"

"We're giving it house room. It's yours. The house of a diplomat's wife can't have a radio ham plaything in it even if he has separated from her. You need it to get your music to London, and you can't do it only by mail because the censors delay everything."

Ann made things so easy that Catherine had to apologize. "I was being too watchful. It was all the holdups about getting here." Delayed action as in bombs, she thought, successfully holding off fear.

"You mustn't worry about possible thieves watching. It would take five major athletes to get this thing out."

"In case it was a flash camera, instead of fireworks. This happens to look suspicious and I very much can't have you involved."

Ann said, "In that case, the thing is to see where it's coming from. Stay inside." She went out into the garden and turned on the lawn sprinkler, spraying by hand so that the water went as far as possible, making peacock-tail fans.

Another burst of light, finished in a second. She climbed over the low hedge and went in the direction of the last flash. Catherine waited. After what seemed a long time, she came back laughing and said to Catherine, "It was no more than Istanbul's usual. Two street boys were trying to have a firework festival. It was horribly dangerous, I thought. They'd pinched a box of rockets that looked as if they dated back to the American Civil War. Most of them were duds because they'd gotten damp. Also the boys were lighting the rockets from the wrong end."

"Where had they got them from?"

"They weren't going to say, but I could see the sign on the box. From Kemal's, wouldn't you know. He bought some from Spain just before the Spanish Civil War but the money went to the Fascists and he's refused ever since to sell anything from fascist sources."

"Did the children know you were Kemal's wife?"

"These kids know everything. They were scared. One of them had some papers that he said he had to deliver and ran away."

"Was he our mailboy? Thomas gets his mail delivered to my place now."

"What does he look like?"

"He usually wears that royal blue sweater of mine. The one Jean-Pierre hated because it drew attention, he said."

"Yes, that was him. What happened to the royal blue trousers it went with, then?"

"Same thing. Jean-Pierre. He really hates women in pants. They were too big for the boy but he took them anyway and I think he managed to sell them to somebody."

"It's all very feudal. Money's not worth anything stable internationally so we've gone back to trading in things."

Ann went out into the garden again.

Catherine turned the knobs of the wireless. Ann moved the antennae, watching Catherine as she nodded at the sound of familiar wavelengths near the one she wanted. Then Catherine nodded vehemently as she hit the "Allo allo allo" call. Going like a music hall routine, the exchange carried cheer as always.

"Allo allo allo."

"Held up for high tea, were you?"

"Gilbert and Sullivan."

"Not exactly you."

"How about the Handel parody in *Trial by Jury?*"

"Pardon?"

"Handel parody in *Trial by Jury*, I said." She sang it. " 'He'll tell you how he came to be a judge.' "

"I'll take you down your particulars, I will."

"Nothing my father wouldn't approve of."

She wrote down seven letters of the alphabet she was given. Vital telephone number. Then she heard, "Ready for composition-dictation. Roger."

She dictated pages of music note by note that she wrote down fast as she was dictating, working from memory, stopping every now and then to recapture exactly what she had in mind. Today she had had no time to write it out first. It was a laborious process. Key signature changes. First the melodic line, then the harmonic line in the bass. It took her three-quarters of an hour. To Ann, her friend's back looked clenched in concentration to the point of pain. She put her hands on Catherine's shoulders as if to weight an imagination that was lifting off the ground. At length it was over.

"Have you finished?" said Ann.

"That part. Then about another ten minutes," said Catherine.

Ann pressed her hands harder onto Catherine's shoulders. "Thank you," Catherine said.

"Who's the other call to?"

"Another radio ham. He's waiting. Hang on. Hell," Catherine said, adjusting her headset. "Ah, there it is. C. G. Come in, C. G."

"C. G. and over. Roger."

Catherine cut off the switch that would have allowed Ann to hear the other end, whispering, "Sorry, I can't get the volume any other way." Then, to the radio, in rapid French, "No, Elise, it's madame, it's for Monsieur Le Chef, 7301520, attach the telephone, dial the number, if you would be so kind. . . . *Cher maître,* news for you, *premier cru,* vintage 1933 . . . straightaway, thirty thousand for St. James's and also three repeat three cocoa poured into steel mugs and four repeat four repeat whole-wheat biscuits in tins and six repeat six repeat *fraises du bois* beautiful if served on sterling silver and nine repeat nine repeat nine copper pennies from your Red Cross box to put toward a Penny Black stamp for good fortune . . . yes . . . a thousand times."

She snapped off all of the switches and sat back for a moment. Ann had left her to herself and found the address of the telephone building from a neighbor. "You wanted this" was all she said.

14

♦

CATHERINE kissed Ann and sped off to find the telephone operator. She expected it to be far more difficult than transmitting her messages to England. The security guard there was asleep and, when she woke him, was disarmingly not angry to be caught napping. He nodded in answer to her explanation and shouted into an intercom in the ugly concrete wall of the lobby. It had been finished just before the War and Catherine had visions of the sick man of Europe's entrails still as poorly as ever, untended and given no professional care, symbolized all too literally in wires and cables not properly attached so that the life-fluid of people's talk was left to pour away and be lost forever. The intercom that the guard used was placed in a position at his waist, too high for kneeling, too low for standing.

"A Bulgarian architect," he said with a venomous flourish at the building. Nothing, Catherine thought, could more have affected Istanbul's attitude to the Axis than this silly building. There was a plaque in gold registering the date of the building's completion, with the self-important signature of the architect in facsimile. It was a name known to her, a Bulgarian who had been key in linking his country to the Axis. The building was heedless of human need and looked smugly sure of its right to seem uncompleted. It was like something ordered by Mussolini over the telephone.

A Turkish girl dismayingly short of breath came rushing down many flights of stairs. The lift was out of order.

"Are you an international operator?" said Catherine, when the girl had stopped panting.

"I am the operator," she said simple. "Ismeta."

"You mean there aren't a lot of you?"

"It's a public holiday, madame." Pause. "On other days there are several of us."

"Then I owe you something for the telephone call I made from the British Council to New York. Do you remember?"

The girl, unusually thin for a Turkish girl, started to cry.

"How much do I owe you?" Catherine said.

"I am not a beggar, madame."

"No, of course not. You're a professional. *I* made the mistake; I'm sure I heard you wrongly."

It took a long time for the truth to be arrived at. Catherine owed the British Council ten times more than she had been told.

"But the billing cannot be changed now," said the operator desperately. "I gave it to you in the hearing of the manager before he was officially off."

"Tell him that you and I were speaking as friends and that I misunderstood. My name is Catherine. Tell him that the accounts people in New York didn't understand our methods, let alone our friendships, Turkey's and France's, and that they questioned me about the charge and the matter is *altogether* one of bureaucracy not comprehending friendship."

Elitism banished, the girl accepted the piastres, which Catherine put into an envelope addressed to "The Manager, by kind hand of Ismeta, Telephone Company, Istanbul."

The guard, again asleep, woke up and saluted, saying in halting English, "Good-night, Catherine Mrs." Since the old

Arabic writing from right to left had lately been changed to European writing from left to right, Catherine had noticed that many of the older people of Istanbul put words backward.

In the dark now, Catherine was running home to Thomas. Late, late, she hated being late. She could hear someone trailing her. In a street of little bazaar shops she had got as far as one that bore the sign "Optician. Checks Cashed. *Official* rates"—by now there existed the "official rate," the "official black market rate," and the "unofficial black market rate"—when she felt her arm being held. Catherine made the immediate connection to the face at the reception where there had been the shot from the silencer gun. Not that Hilda had visibly had anything to do with that, but the long sad face had registered. The grabbing of the arm seemed friendly enough. "You'd better come with me," said Hilda firmly.

"I'm late," said Catherine.

"Better come with me. There are penalties for lateness here."

"Yavash yavash." Catherine tried Turkish. "No hurry." And no response, either. What "here"? Suddenly, a "here" that had nothing to do with this small well-known street. Hilda wheeled her around into the oculist's little shop. There was the usual clanking of wood beads that made the usual shop curtains. Streets away, people were singing to Turkish popular music. It took a moment for Catherine to be able to see anything. The light inside the shop made nothing but a white blur at first. Then she made out a glaucoma test machine in the center of the little room, two men in dark glasses with their hands in their pockets, and of all things a piano. Don't run, don't look suspicious, fix on the piano.

Hilda sat Catherine down at the glaucoma test machine and held her there, quite lightly. Her hands were in the same position as Ann's only a while ago. Catherine suddenly made out the face of Jean-Pierre's valet, Mehmed.

"Mehmed!" she said, suddenly feeling that she could control the situation. "Was it you who drove monsieur to see me?"

Mehmed made no response. Catherine was, as always, haunted by his likeness to an ill-cast *maître d'hôtel*. This time he was going to say that there was no table for her, that they were all booked, and give her no "madame."

"We wear dark glasses on account of the light, not so that you should not recognize us. I am your friend," said Mehmed after his chosen pause.

At last he was in a position not only to emulate her, but to proffer comradeship as a superior. His dream. "And this is my colleague, Klaus Adler."

Catherine attempted to shake hands, which riled the man because he was in the midst of clicking his heels and saying, "Heil Hitler."

She played some scales and said idly in German, "Have you some more dark glasses I could borrow? It's very bright here."

"You speak the language. Excellent. Your eyes will get attuned. We need brightness for the patient in order that we should get proper records." Mehmed laughed at his colleague's wit and then looked anxiously at Catherine, who could muster only a smile in the face of his absurdity.

"Mehmed, would you lend me your dark glasses?" she said to make some consoling link. She spoke in Turkish. He hesitated, and then seemed delighted to be able to confer something on her, though his unshielded eyes could be seen to be watering. No, he was crying. He didn't even appear to mind that she noticed, and held out an arm in her direction for a second for no obvious reason.

"I'm very glad to see you, Mehmed," she said. Again, how odd that this should be the natural thing to say.

"You are unwise to treat him familiarly," said Klaus. "He is not your servant. You are in his debt. He has always been most tactful about your doings."

Hilda put on dark glasses that she had in her pocket and said in English, "Just stare into the machine. Only a moment."

Klaus said to Mehmed. "Is the wire recorder going?"

Catherine looked around and made out a wire recorder that was just like one she had left in Jean-Pierre's keeping in Ankara years ago. "Is that my wire recorder? I remember the serial number. K162704," she said in Turkish. Mehmed brought the wire recorder to her and showed her the model number. It was indeed hers, in working order, and going. "Mehmed brought it especially for our appointment," said Klaus. "It was his idea. He wished to make you know that you were at home."

"Tell us your history," said Mehmed in French, visibly as proud as a child to speak in her born tongue.

"Scarlet fever, measles, chicken pox, German measles, mumps," Catherine said back to him fast.

Klaus said, not understanding much except her swiftness, "Your political history. Are you or have you ever been a member of the French underground?" Trailing her speed, he attempted French.

"I have dual citizenship," said Catherine in German.

"There is nothing funny about evasiveness. We shall try the glaucoma test," he said, backing away into German. She had forced a retreat.

Her chin was strapped to the chin rest of the machine.

"Don't play games. Are you or have you ever been involved in a major French operation?"

144

"Appendicitis."

The lights were turned up still further.

"I can see we're not getting anywhere. Tell us about these notes."

Catherine looked. Something she had crumpled. Her usual shorthand of music notation and letters standing for numbers. Someone plundering her rubbish bin, it seemed. She caught sight of "She calls him the toad" on another big bunch of notes sticking out of Klaus's pocket; her words, but no hand she knew.

"I can't really see in this light. They're something I'm composing."

She was led to the piano, "Play, please," said Klaus.

"I need the notes, and the light turned down."

"You play by touch. Your memory is phenomenal. If it will help you, we will bandage your eyes. We have a trained musician to listen to you. He will help if memory falters."

"Tell me which page number you want me to play."

"Any numbers are your own."

She waited for a moment and thought of Jean-Pierre, of Thomas waiting, of her friends in the underground, of Mozart. Then she played "Dove Sono" from *The Marriage of Figaro*. Mehmed said to Klaus, "That's 'Dove Sono.' It's got nothing to do with what's here."

Catherine now knew what she had to deal with. She had to remember exactly what she had written. "Mehmed, I didn't know you were musically trained."

"I learned much from you," he said. "I listened to everything. I studied your scores. I have a degree now."

She burst out laughing. Oh lord, the unchangeable Mehmed consigned forever to a buffoon's role as her mimic. He was as embarrassed as she was. She concentrated and played. "That's the end of the page you have, I think."

Klaus said to Mehmed, "Correct?"

"The parts in the musical stave, correct. The annotations, incomprehensible. Or Roman numerals."

"They're my way of limbering up." She decided to tell the truth fast, reckoning that Mehmed was not equipped to follow her. "They have to do with temperament. As you know from 'The Well-Tempered Clavier,' Mehmed. The discovery of the essential tuning solution that the seven semitones of a perfect fifth should not be tuned as 7 but as 7.019550008654. The brilliant tiny difference called the Pythagorean comma."

"Riddles?" said Klaus to Mehmed.

"No," said Mehmed brazenly, in the voice that Catherine knew so well. He was faking knowledge as he faked command of anything.

She decided to push further, undid the lid of the piano and plucked A above middle C. Then put her finger halfway on the string. Then redid it and divided the string by a third. "You hear it, Mehmed, of course. The harmonic series. The fundamental, the octave, the fifth." The familiarity of tuning an instrument was comforting. "And one can go on forever, of course, mathematically speaking. As you know from Mehmed, it is possible to break church windows with the vibrations of the upper partials."

"Is this gibberish?" said Klaus to Mehmed.

"Oh no," said Mehmed emphatically.

Coward, thought Catherine.

Klaus returned to the attack. "Our question about operations did not give us an adequate answer. We were asking you about major military operations. Have you ever been involved in major military operations?"

"No," said Catherine.

"Repeat," said Klaus, showing her the swastika behind his coat lapel.

"No," said Catherine.

Klaus took off his coat and tore off the swastika and burned it with a match struck on his heel. So he was frightened, she thought. For all the pressure of Hilda's hands, Catherine felt at liberty. She got up and said, "I should go now." It would be losing ground to ask who had come by the papers, what had been paid for them, how they had been pilfered. She shook hands courteously, first with Hilda, then with the men, including Mehmed.

Mehmed said, "And how is Mr. Drake?"

Catherine clung to the truth and said, "He was at the British Council when I last saw him. They're in the middle of an amateur performance of *Trial by Jury*."

She left the shop, not too late to see Hilda spreading her hands in some gesture of acceptance to the others and nodding satisfaction. Hilda then came to her at the door and again shook her hand and said, "I admire your musicality." Not music. She genuinely meant something greater.

"Thank you."

"A saving grace."

It was a marked moment between the two women. Some quite unexpected salute was being passed by Hilda. Catherine thought about her saddened face as she first walked and then ran to her house.

*T*homas was asleep, diagonally across the bed. He woke up and said simply, "Thank God. I was worried to death." He so obviously meant it that she didn't ask how he had managed to sleep. He proffered the reason. "I thought perhaps you'd left me. Left me forever. I went swimming in the Bosphorus for hours."

"To be alone," she said.

"I was determined to wear myself out and get some

sleep. The jitters isn't a particularly honorable thing to have."

She undressed and put on a white linen nightdress, saying, "Dread's also not up to much. I had that today. This evening."

"Was it about something specific?"

"Yes." She couldn't go further.

"What does it feel like?"

"It's gone now." She smiled at him, visibly, in the dim light reflected from the moonlit Bosphorus. "That would be from being with you." She reached for her Paisley notebook and wrote down three bars of music. "What are you writing?" Thomas said.

"Something I've been humming. I don't want to forget it. How was *Trial by Jury?* I caught a glimpse of your back. You were running and I couldn't catch up with you."

He said, "I got dragged into it by a client at the bank who depended on the place being open." He paused, then said, "Catherine, I must tell you—" But he waited.

"Have a glass of water," she said. "The saltwater will have made your mouth dry." She got him some soda water.

"Darling, you do know I'm ferociously not superstitious," he said. A start.

"It wouldn't be a fault if you were." Catherine left him to tell her what he wanted. Leave people room.

"I was frightened for you. Or frightened about not knowing something I should be aware of. I didn't want to go to anyone you knew. I don't think I'd actually have asked anyone's—counsel—at all if dependable Sukru hadn't suddenly grabbed my elbow and shoved me in the direction of a fortune-teller. Of all things. But it seemed safe enough. I don't know why I didn't ask you directly. I guess I was afraid you're shielding me from knowing something."

"What does she look like?"

"In uniform, so to speak, she looks like a gypsy. In garden-party clothes she looks like Ophelia updated to a Bloomsbury picnic."

"But her face."

"Long and sad."

"Yes, I've met her." Catherine got up and walked around. "Skin of our teeth department, darling. Don't go there again. She's a dangerous woman and I don't think she knows it. The sadness you noticed is the truth, I think, though I've no idea what it's due to. You've probably seen more of her than I have. What do you put it down to?"

"I don't know either."

"What's her place like?"

"It has a little girl running around in it that she seems connected to but not as any mother would be. The woman seems removed. It's not quite irresponsibility, even though the child's terrifyingly small to be left alone. She seems to be Istanbul's common property, like the cats. Probably the world's common property. No one owns the cats, no one seems properly to look after the child, but they somehow get fed."

"That sounds like Istanbul. Have you got children in America?" A crucial pause.

"Two. My wife's remarried. She has custody." Pause. "I didn't tell you because—oh, I guess I didn't want to find you when I was carrying a lot of baggage. The kids are, God help me, elsewhere."

"You miss them."

"Very much. Darling, will you forgive me?"

"No harm's done," she repeated. "All shall be well, and all manner of thing shall be well."

"That's pretty. No 's' on 'thing'?"

"No."

"Could you set it to music?"

It was something that had never occurred to her to try before, though she had said the T. S. Eliot lines to herself often enough. They went downstairs together to the clavichord. She thought for a while and then played a setting for the two lines.

"Why no bass?" said Thomas. "But it's beautiful."

"I was thinking of it for the mandolin."

She thought again, and then showed him five notes in the bass for him to play to sustain the harmony as the treble moved.

"Don't forget it. Write it down," he said.

She smiled at him and said, "It's not something I'll forget."

*T*hey woke early. From habit, she picked up a Chekhov story she had been reading at some lonelier time, then put her arm around his shoulder, looked up at him for a while, and only then down at the page where she had had to leave off. He looked over her shoulders. It was in Russian.

"What are you reading?" he said.

" 'The Lady with the Dog' again." He knew the story. He watched her wriggling her toes, wondering where she had got to. "You write in music, Arabic, whatever our script is, Russian, and Greek for all I know. Though I can't read your writing without a magnifying glass."

"I expect it's because I write as fast as I think. Quite a lot of people can read it. Can you yet?"

"Not always, but I keep all your notes to me in a special pocket."

"Even if you can't understand them?"

"I wouldn't ever throw them away."

"My sister and I have practically identical handwriting

now. It's odd. We used to write differently when we were together all the time, and now that we're apart our writing has grown nearly the same. Our father once told me that a letter to him was so indecipherable that he was thinking of sending it to a chemist as a prescription to be made up."

He lay back, on the eased time she had given him, and said, "What are you?"

"Do you mean what religion? I suppose agnostic, but I'd wish to be Christian. That's to do with birthplace, yes?"

"What else are you?" he said. Pause. They switched tacitly to an agreement to play.

"Physically I'm ninety percent water, a lot of bone, 4.74 litres of blood. Chemically I'm all sorts of valuable commodities that fluctuate interestingly, like iron and potassium."

He was struck. "Fluctuate interestingly?" It made sense to him only as a remark that you might hear from an improbably serene gambler on the stock exchange, so inapt a connection it could have no bearing. Instead he said, "No, I'd rather ask you about your sister. Emma."

"You've noticed our useful pot."

"You're very attached to her, aren't you."

"Yes."

"Where is she?"

"She's married to a German."

"Are you able to write to her?"

There was a very long pause. "It's difficult politically." She couldn't go on. Or chose not to, perhaps.

He finished for her. "He's a Nazi, and she's loyal to him?"

"Roughly that."

She went back to Chekhov. "Drag my mind back into Chekhov, darling," she said after her own attempts had failed.

Their breakfast was brought in to them and she sat up

eagerly for croissants and coffee. Anything to take her thoughts away from Emma. There had been a rumor that she had been hurt in an English air raid on Germany, but every effort Catherine had made through every mutual friend who might have found precise news had come to nothing. Wait, wait, think of the War, think of living things out, think of continuing well. Emma had always continued well. She left options open to people. She liked to treat people with a loose rein.

"Describe her, can you?" said Thomas.

"We're very much the same. To look at. In character, I can only tell you that she has a high sense of honor, and that she carries something festive into a room. She's a great woman." No possibility of a past tense.

Thomas said, "As you."

Catherine shook her head and said instantly, "Oh no, she's much, *much* more than I am." She paused again, and then said, "A grand old woman of France once said about her when she was seventeen that 'her mind has the noble structure of accuracy.'"

There was a very filled silence between them. Then Thomas got up quickly and went to work.

W hen he came back, he found Catherine in the same position but dressed, lying on the now-uncrumpled pile of cushions and speaking on a telephone he had never seen before. She didn't notice him come in. She was speaking in many languages between calls that were made very fast, using words he couldn't grasp even in English. Suddenly she saw him, said some swift parting into the telephone, held her arms out to him.

"Look what we've got. A telephone," she said.

"Does it work?" he said, having got used to Istanbul.

"Perfectly."

"How did you get it? Telephones don't grow on trees. Let alone installed telephones."

"Isn't it peculiar, that saying. Practically nothing grows on trees except leaves. What's more," she said, "it was a present."

"A bribe?"

"*No.* A girl I'd seen at the telephone company yesterday about some money I owed her for a call to America simply turned up today with an engineer to install the beautiful thing. She said she wasn't used to people coming to pay when they hadn't had a bill."

"She's probably in cahoots with the mail-delivery boy."

"Oh no."

"Everybody in Istanbul seems to be up to something."

"Darling, don't be suspicious."

"It's a question of not being gullible."

"Did something bad happen at the bank? You look perturbed."

"It's not that. I think it's the hangover of having been neutral all the time when you're so deeply not."

"Oh love. Yes, you would feel that. It's one of the reasons why you're so dear to me."

"Is that telephone safe?"

"Nothing is."

"How do you manage?"

She thought. "Concentration on balance helps. You've got it, though you don't seem aware. It's a wonder to me, the sense of balance you dispense. You're not—"

The telephone rang. It was Ann, from Kemal's momentarily empty office. He had been rung by Ismeta at the telephone company with a brand-new telephone number. She gave Catherine a message reminding her that a radio transmission was due tonight.

Thomas raised his eyebrows and said, when she put the phone down, "Who's already got the number?"

"Ann Wisner. On the train from France with me. 'A lifetime ago or three seasons, whichever be the longer' or whatever we once said. Not a diplomat, a maid, a stalker or a cobbler or a suspected Nazi. A *friend*. It's like real life."

"Oh, *that* friend. But how did she know you had a telephone?"

"The manager of the city telephone company knows who all the foreigners are in Istanbul. It's not curiosity. He simply counts friendship high. Most Turks do. He knew Ann was a friend. He knew that Kemal had a telephone so he told Kemal that I had a telephone as a thank-you present."

"Is it really that simple?"

"Taking things at face value isn't a bad rule."

Thomas thought he would never understand Catherine sometimes, and said so, not harshly.

She got up and walked about.

"What's on your mind?" he said.

"I was thinking that perhaps one never does understand people and shouldn't try. And that maybe that's why everyone responds to Chekhov. Or one of the reasons. He doesn't expect to explain the order of a temperament. People being different, thank goodness. I reckon the order is always there but no one ever knows the half of it." She looked at the pot of Emma's and hers, and thought once again of all she didn't know about Thomas, of what gave him firm ground, of whom he missed, of what allowed him to fly.

"And in the meantime, there is the very actual beauty of your legs, and the page you've got to in Chekhov," he said.

She picked him up immediately by saying, "And the very

actual fact that I'm due at Ann's in half an hour and haven't got dressed." The other things she hadn't done would have to be achieved below hatches. A matter of allotting tacit work to a silent place in the mind.

At the same time, Hilda, in her guise personifying the occult, was perverting the simple to a truly distressed New Zealand woman concerned about whether or not her husband's affair with his secretary was serious. Hilda had charged her abominably highly for her claimed pipeline to omniscience.

"Ah," she said, with the repetitive promise of balm to come, "we must search here for clues in your character. My cards tell me that you are in deep need of satiety. To love totally one must understand totally. It is the greatest misapprehension of love, to leave things uninvestigated for fear of destroying passion. If one is passionate, one consumes. One consumes the beloved as a boa constrictor consumes a sheep. And then the sheep becomes part of the self. The bulge disappears. One becomes svelte through this very act of appetite." And she ran her hands over her figure, which was indeed like a girl's. The New Zealand woman, who had been lonely for a confidante only to find her self ransacked, rushed out of Hilda's room to be sick in the street.

Hilda watched out of the window, and for once held on to the child. The little girl, intermittently attended to, was Hilda's child by a Brazilian man who had left her suddenly in Turkey without friends, a roof, resources. He had been, once, someone she loved. Now, so far as she knew, he continued his veiled businesses abroad, merging companies, living off graft. Hilda held on to the child not only to stop her from falling but also, in an impulse quite out of her usual character, to stop her seeing such a result of her mother's advertised trade.

15

♦

THOMAS and Catherine were together in the Blue Mosque looking at the icons. Sukru came up to them in Catherine's clothes, proudly worn. The royal blue things disliked by Jean-Pierre, trousers and all, the trousers kept up by a belt that Catherine recognized as a broken luggage strap she had thrown away. It went round him twice, and the trousers were rolled up by a foot at least in the legs. At the waist, they were bunched like a dirndl skirt.

"Your friend the cobbler showed me how to mend your strap, madame," he said in Turkish. "You had no use for it. I have here your mail, and Mr. Thomas Drake's." He also had Hilda's child with him, clutching her by the hand. Her white dress and its drooping petticoat—she silently showed Catherine the broken elastic of the waist-seaming—had traces of the blue of Catherine's discarded trousers.

"This is the fortune-teller's little girl," said Thomas in English to Catherine.

"What happened to her dress?" she said. She squatted down and counted the child's bare toes, and then her own. The child looked gravely pleased that she had ten toes in common with Catherine, and counted both sets herself to make sure.

"I have adopted her," said Sukru. "I washed her dress

with madame's discarded trousers. The colors went into each other nicely."

"Who ironed them?" said Catherine.

"Miss Agnès. I gave her the money you gave me for the delivery to the fortune-teller woman. To tell the truth, I am disgusted with her. She doesn't look after Fram's safety."

"Fram?"

"I have named her after the name at the end of your mail, madame. F.R.A.M. No one else here has this name."

Catherine shook hands with the little girl.

"What are you *talking* about, Catherine?" said Thomas to all this Turkish.

"Thomas, this is Fram," said Catherine in both Turkish and English.

"She looks in safer hands than usual," said Thomas. "Why Fram?"

"Fellow of the Royal Academy of Music."

"I thought you said your cipher-eluding correspondent wrote out your degree in words," said Thomas.

"He's started not to bother now that everyone who notices things like that has taken it in."

She asked Sukru for the letters, and then saw that, among the airmail from her English friends, there was a German-stamped envelope addressed in a hand she didn't recognize. Thomas and everyone else watched her face begin to glow as she looked at the letter. She held it out to Thomas silently.

"A drawing. More code?" he said.

"My sister. She's using her left hand. Someone else must have written the envelope." A nurse? "She's telling me she's alive and that all's well, though something must be wrong with her right hand. Perhaps she's lost it." She flicked her head away. "But she's still *alive*. It's a hurrah drawing we used to do when we were children. She's done it the way I did. I've never been any good at getting the shoulders to fit onto the body. I just used to concentrate on the face and the grin and the right arm going up and the left arm going outward. It's a sign we send each other after long gaps. It means hurrah and bravo. Sukru," in Turkish, "are those papers for us?"

"As I was saying," he said, determined to speak his new English from now on, "Hilda underpaid me, so I am giving the delivery to you after all. Fram has been wearing them in her clothes for you."

"Where she kept the lettuce sandwiches from the British Council?" said Thomas.

"They were perfectly safe there," said Sukru, pointing.

The child nodded in confirmation.

"She came with me to the German Consulate where Hilda had asked for them to be delivered. But Hilda can't be earning enough money from them, I told the German consul. Or else she would be a better mother and also she would have paid me properly."

"You mean that Hilda's employed by the Germans?"

"At the unofficial black market rate. It should be the *official* black market rate. Of course. That is the rate I receive. They must consider her bad at her job."

"Did you tell the German Consulate you refused to make the delivery?"

"Naturally. I reassured the Consul that they were most safe." He looked at Fram. "She was, of course, with me. I had not yet spent the piastres madame gave me on cleaning Fram up so she did not look altogether spick-and-span but she was entirely silent."

Catherine undid the packet. Notes in the same hand as Klaus's one about the toad, and a copy of the seemingly missing German military command pamphlet that the woman she could now identify had handed over so fast to Sukru in the road.

"Then what happened?" she said.

"They offered me any number of piastres I wanted if I left them with Fram but I was not going to allow Fram to come under suspicion. She is by far too young to know anything of these things. And as I am already raw with marks of a beating I received from taking some fireworks, I know that Fram is too young for a beating. I lined her with newspaper in case of such a beating and then there was a rain on the way to the Germans and her dress absorbed the newspaper ink."

"But then what happened?"

Sukru wagged his head. "And then they put me on the telephone. They said the Ambassador himself in Ankara wished to speak to me."

"What did he say?"

"He said it was important to have the papers from Hilda. I said they had already been delivered which was not a lie because I had given them to Fram. He asked where, and I said that was a private matter."

"The delivery to Fram's petticoat pocket," said Thomas.

"I withheld the knowledge entirely," said Sukru. "Fram can say that I am right. The Ambassador and I were speaking Turkish."

Fram nodded.

"So *then* what happened?" said Catherine.

"The Ambassador was cross. I have noticed several times that several German people get cross."

"Madame's husband's driver does," said Thomas.

"Ah, Mehmed," said Sukru. "He has a magnificent temper. I never expected so much. He was with the Consul.

159

The Consul was cross but not so much. And then the Ambassador was more cross."

"Was anyone else cross?" said Catherine.

"Hilda was cross," said Sukru.

"At what particular stage?" said Thomas.

"She was cross when I told her that I had taken Fram's dress to be ironed at your house. That was before the Consul was cross. And then later she was cross like an earthquake with the Ambassador."

"An earthquake," said Thomas.

"We have many earthquakes in Turkey. Things spill out of the mountains that are dangerous. They cause trouble."

"When you were visiting Hilda, where was Fram?" said Catherine.

"She was in the safe hands of the Chinese manservant at Mr. Thomas Drake's other house," said Sukru. "He supplied us with the newspaper. Newspaper is famous for its warmth as well as for its helpfulness if one is beaten. Fram would have been cold with her dress wet."

"And how is the Chinese manservant?" said Thomas.

"He says he is very well and sends you his regards."

"When you were there, did you happen to see any striped blue and white shirts?"

"Your manservant is wearing a fine blue and white shirt freshly laundered every time I see him," said Sukru.

"Do you see him often?"

"Oh yes. He has kept asking me about the newspaper and asked me to bring it to you. Then he told me he was not being paid by the bank any longer so I advised him to cut up the newspaper and sell it for souvenirs. He has done the same thing with many pages of this stupid official pamphlet. The Ambassador himself said that the pamphlet was entirely a bungle and most stupid. He said this while he was being cross and afterward also."

"About this pamphlet," said Thomas to Sukru, man to man. "The cut-up one."

"The pieces are quite small but he hangs them on his supply of silver chains. I believe he took them from Mr. Kemal when Mr. Kemal decided not to trade with Spain anymore because of loyalty."

"Took them?"

"It was quite all right. No one saw, so no harm was done."

Thomas went over to the line of shoes at the entrance to the Blue Mosque, stripped off the insole of one of his own shoes, and came back with a baffled look.

"Catherine, help," he said. "You can manage," she said.

"Sukru," Thomas said, "do you happen to have seen a note that was gummed inside my shoe for safety?"

"Your secretary at the bank was asking about it. She said that Hilda had been asking her whether she had anything with *peculiar* marks. I noticed marks on the map with the arrow I safeguarded. Immediately, I told her that I understood very well from other papers I handle."

"Did you divulge the source?" said Thomas as calmly as possible.

"As Hilda is your bank's client I thought it best to be helpful but I gave no names. That is not her business."

"So where is the note now?" said Thomas to Catherine.

Catherine said to Thomas, "Which note are we speaking about?"

"The reliable secretary's gummed-shoe note."

Sukru picked up Fram's skirt and handed Thomas the map, much stained with newsprint and rain and then with the blue of his trousers. Catherine looked at her notes on the back and said to Thomas, "This isn't the phrase book ransom note. It isn't the one you said you'd get gummed. Look in the other shoe. Has your secretary got gumming habits?"

Thomas went back to his other shoe and came back with his hands spread.

"Sukru," he said in a senior voice, "the note we are actually looking for now would have been in the *other* shoe you opened. I am sure you were reliably opening both shoes on our behalf. Probably while we were asleep."

"I thought of that duty at once, sir. One shoe or both shoes. Not reliable places." Fram's petticoat pocket was again delved into and the ransom note was found. It was quite unreadably smudged with blue and newsprint.

Sukru said, "Her petticoat, wet because of the newspaper, was washed by me at the same time as the trousers. It was stained all over already but washing made it no better."

"Those blue trousers can obviously only be dry-cleaned," said Thomas to Catherine.

"I know," said Catherine, looking at the inner label hanging out of the back of Sukru's bunched waistline. "It says so. *Nettoyage à sec.*"

"Though *nettoyage* is making clean, isn't it?" said Thomas. "De-dirtying. As one might *nettoyer* one's hands."

"But one wouldn't *nettoie* them *à sec*," said Catherine.

Thomas gathered himself. "So what are we left with?"

"Skin of our teeth," said Catherine. Fram obligingly emptied out the pocket of her petticoat onto the marble floor of the Blue Mosque. Many other things of less value emerged. Thomas and Catherine picked the detritus up for inspection and returned them for sober safekeeping by Fram again, at the same time wondering what else was hanging in piecemeal souvenir form on silver chains stolen from Ann's husband's storeroom of goods from Franco's Spain that he thought to have written off in his anti-Fascist decision.

Everyone shook hands. Thomas and Catherine and Sukru and Fram walked softly out of the Mosque.

16

♦

"AND now it starts to get adult again," said Thomas to Catherine.

"You were thinking of your kids."

"No, of me, I'm afraid. I realize I'm privileged now but as a child I happened to be handed about rather like Fram. My elder sister really looked after me."

"Not your parents?"

"They separated. I was the younger and I was taken with my mother. My brother was at school and stayed with my father. I ran away when my mother remarried and she thought I was with my father and he thought I was with my mother."

"Where were you?"

"Living off the ground. People manage on very little."

"Didn't your parents *ask* each other?"

"They weren't on speaking terms. They had this thing that it's dislocating for the children of broken homes to see their real mother getting on okay with their real father. It's a mistake, because the fondness usually lasts. But my ex-wife's learned the same dogma. Arm's length."

"Why do people say that childhood's the happiest time of your life?"

"Mine seemed to last forever," said Thomas. "I knew the grown-ups were deceiving themselves about that. One can't wait to be out of it. Everyone's been a child once. Don't they remember that it was mostly terrible and often unjust? No one ever believed what you were trying to say. Except *my* sister. The great thing was seeing each other again. The grown-ups must have noticed that. But all the time they still went on saying, 'You'll look back on this time and wish it had lasted for always.' "

"It's the part they forget."

"You don't."

"Nor do you," he said. "Good about Emma. Very good."

She held a silence.

"Not that good, you're saying," he said.

"Oh no. It's unbeatable. We're just so far away from each other and maybe she's quite badly wounded. I'm almost certain that's what she was telling me."

"But she said hurrah. You've got to carry that out."

"She would say hurrah, whatever. She always did say hurrah and bravo. That's the way we do it. It's a signal that we're making contact. That's what the hurrah's about. And in her case the bravo would be about looking ahead. It's the point when other people say 'Courage' or 'Plug on.' They make you feel you've got forever to go, though. Whereas she says you're already there and keep at it. That's one of the things about her."

There was such pining in the air for a confidence to pass that Thomas had the power to take over and persuaded her to come with him to Ann Wisner's. He knocked on the side of his nose to her as he did it.

"*T*o the home of Music, tra-la-la," he said. "Wherein all Delphos may dwell."

"Is that what they say about music in Virginia? In England it's "What passion cannot music raise and quell." Dryden. He meant that music makes the passions spacious. At least Handel and Purcell assumed that, and they'd know." She hummed.

"I made it up," said Thomas. "I say dwelling and you say quelling."

She asked him to sing what he'd said at the beginning.

"Dammit, I only *said* it. There isn't a tune."

"Then it doesn't work."

"What?"

"I just thought you'd expressed the special relationship. That is what they call it, isn't it? The alliance between America and England?"

"You're French."

"Oké." And she shook her head, though smiling. He'd let down a hope.

"Darling, you've got to tell me what you're up to," said Thomas, on base.

She shook her head.

"You'll go nuts."

"Don't hand me out cant about repressing something. Please."

"It's not cant."

"All right. But in English it really is pronounced can't, and I really *can't*."

He was on the point of shaking her and then thought only about the force of that apostrophe, which struck him into silence. The moment was as absurd, and as potently dangerous, as the moment he had had about her shotgun at Göreme long ago. All he could do was ask her candor in his mind, and hope that she knew that mind.

At Ann's Thomas met her again at last after what seemed a long friendship.

"Ann, Catherine's not able to tell me something and perhaps you can. I think it's important," he said.

Ann looked at Catherine, who shook her head, and then back at Thomas. Cutting preliminaries, she said, "I've been a witness and a troubled one but I only know what I've been allowed to hear."

"Who from?"

"Catherine. There's a lot of gossip but I don't let it get to me."

"I saw Catherine shake her head at you just then," said Thomas.

"She was telling me not to guess."

"And that's the truth," said Catherine.

"Hey. Ann. The pressure on her is more than I think she can cope with and it's going to go on."

"There isn't any," said Catherine. "Ann, he is concerned. Very. Show him the wireless."

The cloth and knickknacks and art books were taken off. Thomas knew a radio ham's transmitting equipment when he saw it. "I built a radio crystal set when I was eleven," he said. "I thought I'd invented the wheel. This thing seems to be stuck at a square."

"I'm not mechanically minded at all," Catherine said.

"That determined vagueness."

"How far did your crystal set transmit?" she said. Nettled at last, she was getting him somewhere.

"Half a mile."

"This set does a hell of a lot more."

Ann saw trouble, and no relief in coffee. She took Catherine by the shoulders and said, "Darling, I do believe you should trust us."

Catherine said, "I do."

"To love, honor and to obey."

"In richness, in poorness." She said it with such thought that Thomas believed he had hit on some further clue. "Catherine, I want to talk to Ann alone. That's firm. Will you go upstairs and rest? May she, Ann?"

Catherine said, "There's a sofa in here. Could I stay down with you? I *am* tired. That's true. I've been running round like a maniac."

It was a glad revelation to hear from someone who seemed to Thomas never to waver in her repose. Catherine lay on the sofa and went into a sleep much like the one she remembered from early childhood, when she had been frightened of nightmares caused by the hooting of owls at night and her father had moved her into his dressing room where she had slept lightly, encased in soft familiar talk between her parents. "Before everything splintered," supplied her grown-up mind. So she dreamed then that the whole planet was dispersed and glassy, scattered with sharp splinters. Dreaming more deeply, she remembered a game that Emma and she had played together long ago of shutting their eyelids and concentrating so that all flickers and molten colors faded and one or the other child—it didn't matter which—could honestly say that all she could see now behind her eyelids was pure whiteness.

She rose to the surface after a time like a fish and Thomas's hand was on her.

"Is it that the bank statements aren't balancing?" he said, of all things.

She laughed and said, "I'm fine."

"Something to do with figures, though." A lull while he thought. "Lucre *is* filthy. And a dread. Unknown dread, like before exams. I get it even though I'm handling other people's money."

"Yup," she said, so fast that he knew she shared something he had said then.

"You know those coins you keep in the frozen beans package in the icebox freezer," he said. She didn't comment. It didn't matter how he knew. "Are you scared of going broke?" he said.

"Aren't we all."

"They're in a lot of currencies. Some are very out-of-date."

"Emma and I had them when we were imagining a trip round the world. With Papa in the diplomatic service we thought we could go anywhere. We were on his laissez-passer in those days. Then we discovered we couldn't."

She sat up.

Ann said, "We both think you should trust us to the hilt. We know you're in danger and you just mustn't be alone."

"I'm not. You're both here. My friends." She walked about. "Friendship's another thing that doesn't grow on trees."

"Darling, show me what's going on about the dumb keyboard," said Ann.

"You got interested in commodities suddenly awhile ago," said Thomas. "It's all right. You're not under questioning. It's us."

"The radio ham thing is to a way through to de Gaulle, isn't it?" said Ann. "What was C. G.?"

"The initials of the Free French Government's address in London. Carlton Gardens."

"And you can't tell Jean-Pierre, and you don't want to implicate even us."

"In what?" said Catherine, looking out at the rambler roses for resolve.

"C Major. C Minor. B Major. B Minor. They stand for commodities, don't they?" said Thomas.

She nodded. "In the order memorized from the financial indexes." Be truthful, be opaque. "That is, taking the first as the initial of the first semitone in the Phrygian mode." Don't let them be party. Pray not.

"Come *on*," said Thomas.

"The overtones you talked about once. In music," said Ann to Catherine.

"The number of vibrations in any note," said Catherine.

"I don't understand a thing but it's all figures," said Ann.

Catherine turned round and said, "Music theory's terribly simple if you're interested but I do know most people aren't. I can't grasp a thing about electricity and can't make myself want to. I once mended a fuse with picture-hanging wire and an electrician said I could have burned the place down because picture-hanging wire is copper. Apparently copper either conducts phenomenally or doesn't conduct at all well. One or the other."

As she genuinely didn't know and was genuinely amazed that it mattered that she should, Thomas started to laugh. "You're the first man I've told that to who didn't get grim with me," she said.

"You deal in copper," said Ann. "I've heard you mutter it on the radio in spite of my rotten grasp of French."

"That must have been when it was low in South Africa but high everywhere else," said Thomas, improvising fast. "Iron?"

"Iron's crucial," said Catherine. "Steel. Munitions. They're calling in all the iron railings and old gates in England to melt down so as to build a barricade round the beaches. It would stop the Nazis for a short while."

"And of course the modulations that your friend and you make in your music have to do with changes in the world market values," said Ann.

"Modulations, fluctuations," said Thomas.

"Mostly the world *black* market value," said Catherine.

"But the official black market," said Thomas.

"Sometimes official, sometimes unofficial, sometimes the actual exchange rate if it's still quoted on the stock exchange. It depends," said Catherine. "Whichever works. Whatever I can get."

"Get. Getting England on the wireless is a miracle in itself. Getting a million dollars' worth of iron by gentleman's agreement is something else," said Thomas. "And I don't even begin to grasp the overtones."

"I explained, but one forgets. Any note sets off a series of overtones or harmonics or upper partials, though they're not exactly the same thing. Anyway. C sets off the C above, the G above that, the C above that, the E above that, dividing to infinity. And *equal* temperament, not the one the Greeks used. But their Phrygian mode giving us the arrangement of tones and semitones all the same. Not the Mixolydian, say."

"Temperance," said Thomas, kissing her. "Well, it's one way of summoning you up, I guess. The Mixolydian's on its own as far as I'm concerned. *Catherine!*"

She sat with her hands in her lap, silent.

"Catherine," he said, "half an explanation really is as good as the complete one to people who don't know musical theory. Couldn't you just *half* go on?"

She said, "I can't think. Just then you—when you said 'summon you up' it sounded as if you were going away and taking a photograph with you."

"The bank says the draft papers aren't near me yet but apparently they need me back on war duty. I've got to go to Ankara first."

Catherine shivered like a dog and said, "Was all this a prelude to that sentence? To the most important sentence? You waited all this time to say it? Why?"

Ann put the headphones on and said, "It's the signal. I thought I heard it." Catherine leapt to the wireless and at the same time said to Thomas again, "*Why?*"

Thomas said, "I don't believe it is the most important sentence in your scale of things. Look at the way you jumped at once to the wireless."

"Hang on. Hang on," said Catherine to England on the wireless and to Thomas at the same time.

He saw that he was splitting her in half and felt that all he could do was kiss the nape of her neck. "I'll be back," he said.

"When?" she said, taking off the earphones.

"You've work to do," he said. Sarcasm was not in his range any longer. "I accept that, for whatever reason you won't explain."

"When you run through it you'll find that I've told you everything," she said.

There was a piercing moment between them before he left. She adjusted the headphones again. Ann stood behind her. To keep her bearings, to try to keep him with her somehow, Catherine shouted after him, "Why can't you trust me? We exist. How can you call me to account?"

When the transmission was over and another pile of music paper written out from memory and played on the dumb keyboard with its tracing paper registering the struck notes, Catherine left Thomas space for himself and then went back to the empty house on the Bosphorus. Even Françoise and Agnès were off. Avoiding looking at the wardrobe that she knew would be without Thomas's things, she lay facedown on the bed of cushions with one arm stretching across the space where Thomas slept. She went into another doze. Then she roused herself and reached for her Paisley notebook. The telephone. She rang Mary Heron at the British Council and asked her if she would be a trooper and try calling her New York friend on the *Wall Street Journal* again. She said she had given her godchild the number of her birthday in Roman numerals and thought she'd better have it in Arabic. Another coded commodity deal accomplished. The market had changed, the wireless transmission had told her. Using her head, she worked out a profit by passing the deal through many countries where she had built up a chain of Allied colleagues. She spoke in many languages, lying back under the sheets that Thomas had felt himself to be drowning in when he first floundered at the bank doing this very work, lost for lack of regular hours and an upright desk chair. I can't go on, I shall go on, hurrah, bravo, it must be possible.

17

♦

THOMAS dealt with his business in Ankara, and then made an appointment to meet Jean-Pierre de Rochefauld, found with some difficulty through the French Embassy. He was in a study in an old house, writing. Hands were shaken.

"It was good of the embassy to give you my address," said Jean-Pierre. "I'm not officially acceptable, of course, having quietly withdrawn myself from representing Vichy. You could call me a neutral, but I am a very small power."

Thomas, startled, kept his eyes away from the desk. He had no wish to see whatever Jean-Pierre was doing.

"I'm keeping up my archives of Turkish history," said Jean-Pierre. "One day they will be of use. I should also have said that it was good of you to come."

Thomas shouted, "Your wife, your ex-wife, is alone, you don't ask about her, you even know all about me but you have the idleness to be polite to me. It's savage."

"To her, you mean."

"Of course."

"You would know."

"You don't even ask why I'm here."

"It goes without saying," said Jean-Pierre.

"No wonder she hates you."

"That's not true."

"Then you must hate her."

Jean-Pierre shook his head and said, surprisingly, "I think you don't know how much she cares for you. May I play you a wire-recording? It's most private. The new Ambassador of course now has an open line to her new telephone."

"You mean a bugged line. Does she *know?*"

"Turkey dislikes fascism and anti-Semitism but at the same time Turkey preserves neutrality. It's on the safer side that she not be aware. We have to be mannerly. Turkey is in a most difficult position."

He played the wire-recording to Thomas, who heard his own voice of a week or two ago to his secretary. "This is Mr. Drake. Transmit to New York as follows, please. 'In answer to message received today making bookings.' And dear, *make* the bookings, will you? Bookings. You know the word to use. *Hay.* 'Making *hay.*' Look everything up in what we call the Girl Scout book in the safe." At the same time there had been the sound of Catherine's voice below Thomas's, and he heard it now for the first time. "Darling," she had been saying softly, "you can't hear me now, and thank God you don't know anything. You're not involved, and thank God for that too. You don't even know that I love you."

It was the end of the spool. Jean-Pierre switched off the machine after the blankness.

"Tampered with?" said Thomas. Jean-Pierre shook his head.

"Thank you for playing it to me. Why did you?"

"Because I don't believe you understand my wife."

"Her last words to me were 'How dare you call me to account.' Or maybe 'How can you.'"

Jean-Pierre cracked his fingers and said, "It makes a difference."

Thomas spread his hands. "She was beside herself. But she wouldn't come with me."

Jean-Pierre said, "You can confide, if you wish. With all safety." He laughed then and said, "I'm too lowly to be bugged."

Thomas said, "I don't understand. It's contradictory and she's not. Yes, I do think she loves me very much. But she chooses to make me go. She must know I love her."

"She's in a contradictory position." Jean-Pierre waited quite a long time and then added, "Possibly we are all—fond. You could make allowances for that possibility, couldn't you?"

"That endless secret money-market dealing all over the world. She isn't a woman after all."

Jean-Pierre was angry, and then the telephone went. Someone else answered for him. It gave him time to recover level. He offered Thomas some coffee.

"That endless coffee, too. But yes, thank you."

Jean-Pierre made a gesture to him that was oddly like a toast. "My wife, or estranged wife, has a talent, you see. She has something of mathematical genius. Which has quickly come, with the War, to financial genius. For a man like yourself, in your profession, it may not always go with loving. Not in a woman. For her it can. There exists the possibility that you will come to recognize this. That you will come to see many things differently. In your case I believe so."

Pause. Thomas watched him, not interrupting.

"Just as she recognized that the political separation between us did not, for me, go with having her as a wife. She is deeply committed at the moment to using her financial brain. And as you know, she is also passionately musical. These passions have come together now and she has put them to high purpose in making money for de Gaulle's resistance."

"You know that for sure and stand aside?"

175

"I know no details. You must have guessed the substance."

"O.K., I flinched it." Thomas suddenly stood, went behind his chair and lifted it to drop it again on the floor, leaning heavily on the arms. "Your *restraint!* If I *didn't* put two and two together and make twenty, like you, it would have been for fear of the risk she's in. Which seems to mean nothing to you."

"It means everything."

"Bullshit. Not from the way you behave."

"People are different, thank God."

"I believe you really *are* guessing." Thomas stamped the chair again. "Catherine's life can't be left to guesswork. She wouldn't trust even me with the answers."

"The trust is implicit. You heard the wire-recording. We cannot tax or pry, Mr. Drake. She has every feeling for the positions of all of us. As to myself, I have no intention of letting political differences, or the existence of your love for each other, constrain the possibilities open to any of us. The possibilities of change."

"Change! What about a resolution?"

Jean-Pierre moved in his chair. "There is no resolution at the moment. But there remains something better, which is resolve. Personal alliances will take their course. This is a terrible war, my friend, and we are all in it. As we shall be in any next wars, irrevocably. It may be that the most deep-running war will be against attrition. Our sense of the past, the historical consciousness through reading that is our stamina, those are already at risk. Technology will go on flourishing but it will not be a reign of mind. We shall simply be, given the fortune of existence, a great many billion citizens of a not exemplary planet. In the meantime, in this war, a sunlit woman has had the courage to enter it in mufti and behave with great purpose on the assumption that she must act entirely alone. Without either of us. She has come into it with her private resources, and I do not mean money. Someone's talent is their most particular property, wouldn't you say?"

IN the eighties, Thomas at 74 was at the height of his career as a nuclear physicist. After the War he had gone back to Harvard to study. He developed a first-rate research mind. The fortieth birthday that he had once found such a signal threat to the innovative had gone by without his noticing it, until his children had broken into his work in the laboratory with a singing telegram warbled on record by a service of the telephone company. He pursued nuclear research that became celebrated and then, at sixty-odd, bent his mind entirely to investigative propositions for a group of concerned ecologists and environmentalists. He had never remarried. Catherine remained unforgettable.

One day in the eighties, he acted on his long-bedded craving to find her. He rang French functionaries in Washington. An official told him—after much testiness about archive questions needing to be put in writing to Paris, and a cutoff while she attended to the breakdown of a FAX machine that fed her documents from Paris in five minutes—that there had been no Jean-Pierre de Rochefauld in Turkey in 1939, 1940, 1941, 1942. Indeed, said the official, there had been no diplomatic relations between Turkey and France during the time from June 1940 to December 1942. *Mais naturellement, monsieur. Le grand tout. La guerre. Je ne me revient pas. Service, monsieur. Je suis pressée.*

Not at all, said the fourth Turkish historian to whom he talked. There had been no break whatever in diplomatic relations between Turkey and France during the past world war.

So Vichy had been blotted out of France's history? And Jean-Pierre with it? And what of Catherine?

Hell-bent, he went to Paris. *Ah, M. de Rochefauld. Oui, absolument, pas de question.* The author, recipient as you know of the Légion d'Honneur and the recognition of the Académie; the author of the great four-volume history of fascism, *c'est-à-dire* antifascism, published first in English as you understand and now crowned with the highest of esteem in French. M. de Rochefauld himself, he died in retirement; only last year, so soon after French publication; but his grave, yes, it is heaped with flowers freshly laid each Sunday.

And of his wife, exclaimed an old French banker whose name Thomas well recollected, surely Mr. Drake knew of her present body of work in England? The famous composer?

In London, he found that the young knew of her best as a campaigner for nuclear disarmament. But that was back in the sixties. And wasn't there some old pop record that kept on being played again, now that there was this revival of the sixties? So said the voters for Thatcherism, having no rage in their hearts about the dismantling of the sixties' great Welfare State.

Thomas pursued. An accomplished guitarist with long, spade-shaped fingernails thought for a flash and played him a tune that was the melody she had written for the mandolin in his presence in Turkey long ago. "Top of the pops, my darling," said the guitarist. "Hit the charts in 1962 a while after she'd used it in a guitar sonata for the greatest guitarist we have. Best not give out her address, she keeps her privacy, but you'll find her any day of the week at seven in the morning around Foreign Office Green."

From the top of a bus in Trafalgar Square Thomas saw her through Admiralty Arch. She was playing the piano at an open-air concert for people before they went to work. She was under banners supporting radicalism's new urgency in England. Perhaps Jean-Pierre had come to terms with that before he died.

Two women in front of him on the bus glanced round at her.

"Look," said one, pointing. "There she is."

"Must be getting on."

"I've got a lot of time for her myself."

*T*homas got off the bus and went Catherine's way. To listen to what she was playing, as a start.